THE LADY'S CROWN

ROYAL COURT SERIES

ANNE R BAILEY

Edited by
VANESSA RICCI-THODE

Inkblot Press

For my husband, who always stands by my side.

PROLOGUE

1533

"You foul b—"

The glare she turned on her husband, Henry Grey, stopped him in his tracks. He staggered a moment later and grabbed onto the table to steady himself.

Frances's attention moved to the shattered glass before the fireplace. Another precious heirloom lost. She focused on the glass to keep her own anger in check. There was no point arguing with him when he was like this. Her husband was a drunk and an imbecile, but mostly he was a disappointed man who clung to his dreams.

"I'll send you away from court. Yes, that's what I'll do."

"And what will that achieve?" She couldn't help herself from lashing out at him.

The threat was very real; as her husband, he could send

her wherever he wanted, but she did not mind being sent home to Bradgate.

"I won't have to see your simpering face and be reminded of your failure to procure me a position on the King's council."

She rolled her eyes. He was being absurd. Had he forgotten she had no power to give him what he wanted? Perhaps he had deluded himself before their marriage into thinking that marrying the King's niece would help him climb the ranks.

Frances pulled at the black stitches of her sleeves; she had other things to worry about. Tomorrow was her mother's funeral, and she would play the part of the chief mourner, and then, perhaps, she would escape to Bradgate and give her husband the reprieve he so desired.

Women weren't highly regarded these days. Just a few weeks ago Queen Catherine had finally been tossed aside. Her crime was having produced only one living child — a useless girl.

Now the distasteful Anne Boleyn sat on her throne.

The world was unfair but this was no surprise to her.

PART I

— TEN YEARS EARLIER —

CHAPTER ONE

1522-1523

As SHE RAN, she could only get glimpses of the sky and the manor behind her. The golden stalks whipped at her face as she ran with increasing haste to get away from the house. When they had arrived at Westhorpe to escape the sweat in London, the wheat had barely reached her knees.

This wasn't what she dwelled on as she ran — her mind was focused on escaping the mournful cries of her mother. Westhorpe was supposed to be a paradise — a safe refuge for them — but now her brother was dead. Had it been her fault?

This thought made her run even faster. Her gown held up in her hand like a peasant girl, her headdress fallen off somewhere. She wanted to run and never be found.

A stone jutting out of the ground sent her flying face first into the ground.

She coughed up dirt and wiped away the debris that stuck to her face. She was finding it hard to breathe now. There was a shooting pain in her ankle. Finding herself unable to stand, she wrapped her arms around her knees and started crying.

She thought of the words she had said to her brother two days ago. How she wished he would disappear and leave her alone. She was terrified that she had placed some curse on him and now he was truly gone.

He was her friend. She hadn't cared that their parents had seemed to prefer him. They played games together and had their own secret code that they used to pass messages to each other. That was all gone now.

Sometime between her sobbing and regrets she had fallen asleep, utterly spent in the wheat field. When she awoke she was confused about where she was. The first time her eyes fluttered open she saw a vision of blue and gold. The sun reflecting through the stalks of wheat. She was completely engulfed by the rich yellow shoots.

She remembered how she had planned to run for the forest and live there with the fairy folk. She propped herself up on her elbows. Her ankle still hurt but not as badly as before. Her dress was definitely ruined though. She froze when she heard a hissing sound coming towards her. Was that a snake?

Suddenly, the field no longer seemed so welcoming and beautiful.

She opened her mouth to scream out but another hissing sound stifled her cry in her throat. She whipped her head to the right thinking she heard rustling.

Finally, she inhaled and let out a cry for help.

But who was around to hear her? Surely, she was going to die — eaten by a giant snake, but no less than what she deserved.

Now there was definitely the sound of something moving through the wheat. Frances gave a yelp as she was overtaken by a big grey dog. It licked her face and barked happily. With a great sense of relief, she recognized it as one of her father's hounds — she had named him Jasper after the woodsman who had brought in the yule log and had a head of grey hair as grey and wild as the dogs'.

"What happened to you, Frances?"

Her father's bulking form was looming over her now. She couldn't make out his face. He was merely a dark shadow, but after a moment's hesitation, she reached out to him.

"Papa."

He crouched beside her, examining her ankle.

"Why did you run away from your nurse?"

"I—I... Mother was so sad." Frances found herself choking on an explanation. "I fell, there was a snake for sure but Jasper scared it away."

She heard her father sigh heavily. "I don't think there was any snake. Come, this is no time for your childish antics."

He scooped her up in his arms with ease and began walking back to the manor. Frances watched Jasper trotting beside her father, a great lolling grin spread on his face as, every once in a while, he would go running off after some rabbit or mouse that caught his attention.

She wished she could be just as carefree as him.

"Papa, what will happen to Henry?" The question was

7

burning in her mind, and she couldn't keep herself from asking.

"He will go to Heaven and we shall pray for his soul."

Frances could see how his eyes went dark and his face seemed to have sunken with renewed grief.

Another question was burning in her mind, but she couldn't bring herself to ask if he wished she had died instead of Henry.

Rather than risk hearing his answer, she clutched her arms around his neck tighter.

~

"His name is Henry."

Frances's hold on her younger sister's hand tightened as she regarded the bundle in her mother's arms.

She had not gone into confinement with her mother, as she was still too young, but she was old enough to understand that her mother would emerge with a new sibling for them. Still she was shocked to hear that her parents had chosen to name their new son after her departed brother.

"For the King, his uncle," her mother continued as if reading her mind.

"He very small," Eleanor babbled as she examined the pale creature.

"He is very small," Frances corrected but Eleanor ignored her.

This little meeting was interrupted by their father's sudden arrival with an arm full of gifts. When he kissed Frances on the cheek she could smell the wine on his breath. He had been celebrating the arrival of his heir for two days now.

He turned away from her.

"How is the little Lord today?" He peered down at his newest son.

"Strong and, God willing, continuing to thrive," Mary smiled up at her husband.

Gently, he picked up the swaddled baby and walked with him around the room. Frances followed his every movement. With every smile and cooing noise, she felt her heart tighten as if someone was gripping it in their hands.

She knew this new baby boy was important. He was her father's heir, but why did it seem like he loved him more?

Ever since the death of Henry a little over a year ago, her father had been distant with her. He had doted on her mother when she was with child and now seemed to devote all his attention to this new son. Was Henry easily forgotten and replaced? Was she so unimportant that they could ignore her?

She bit her lip to stop herself from crying. That would only get her sent away from her parents. She couldn't suppress the fresh swell of bitterness she felt towards the pale creature in her father's arms.

When the baby gurgled, he was handed back to the wet-nurse to be fed.

"I shall go hunt you a stag for your dinner!" Charles pronounced, kissing his noble wife.

"Papa, can I come too?" Frances had gotten quite good on her pony.

But he was already half way out the door by then and

had not seemed to hear her. Deflated she looked to her mother who was fixated on the feeding baby.

"Come along, Ladies." Their nursemaid led her and her sister back to their rooms.

Eleanor was still too small for lessons, but Frances was confined to the school room learning Latin, French and music. She excelled at none of these, much to the dismay of her teacher, Doctor Skeron. He berated her that she did not apply herself for she had excellent parentage. Her mother amazed the court with her skill playing the lute and clavichord.

Whenever Frances stumbled over her French, he would chastise her, saying that she was bringing shame upon her mother who was the Dowager Queen of France, no less.

Deciding his pupil was too distracted today for proper lessons, he let her go back to the nursery with her younger sister. There, Frances was subjected to endless needle work. She almost wished she was back in her mother's room looking at the baby.

"You are using the wrong thread. It will have to be redone."

Frances cringed at the words and frowned as she watched the nurse pluck apart the crude stitches she had done.

"If you don't focus you shall never learn."

Frances wanted to stick out her tongue at the nurse but held herself in check. She didn't need to be scolded or punished for bad behavior. She was no longer her father's favorite and certain he would laugh at her antics.

CHAPTER TWO

1527

SUFFOLK PLACE in the spring time was lush and beautiful. The gardens were always meticulously maintained. Frances was sure her mother had all the flowers planted to keep the smell of London out of their house.

It was a cloudy day and she decided to chance a walk around the garden. She turned to her companions with an air of authority and told them of her plans.

"We shall take a stroll through the gardens today."

It didn't escape her notice the way they threw hidden glances at each other, but Frances was not concerned. After all, who were they to her? They had been brought to Suffolk House to complete their education in the household of the Duchess of Suffolk and to be her companions.

Frances took this to mean they were her inferiors, and, perhaps by breeding they were, although they tended to excel her at dancing and music. So she never forgot to take the opportunity to enforce her authority over them.

After all, she was the King's niece, her mother had been the Queen of France, and she was the daughter of a Duke. They were mere daughters of knights in her father's service.

Her mother had done them a favor taking them in.

Frances always walked before them, maintaining some level of precedence, but she still enjoyed conversing with them.

"Is it true your great-grandmother was Elizabeth Woodville?"

"Yes, she was a descendant of the Royal house of Burgundy," Frances said, her chest puffing out proudly.

Louise sniggered. "And a squire."

Frances stopped in her tracks. "What did you say?"

"Her father was a mere squire. I heard she only married the King through witchcraft."

"It's true. Her mother was convicted of being a witch, and she was only saved because the King was bewitched himself and forgave her," Madeline chimed in.

"That is not true," Frances spat. "It's nothing but lies. I shall tell my mother you have been slandering my family. Perhaps the King will have you thrown into the Tower."

Louise blanched but Madeline only shrugged.

"We can't be in trouble for telling the truth." She studied Frances with a critical gaze. "Perhaps you are a witch too. My mother says you can tell if the person has a blemish. Don't you have one on your right shoulder?"

"It's a beauty mark. I am not a witch."

"Maybe," she replied with a shrug.

Frances was ready to throw a fit but what could she say

to make them believe her? She would speak to her mother. This was unacceptable.

"I wish to continue walking alone. You shall walk five paces behind me," she huffed.

They did as she asked them to.

The matter was dropped for a week, but Frances found her hand reaching for the mark on her right shoulder. Was it really the mark of a witch? She prayed more fervently and never took her eyes off the priest during mass. Surely, a witch would burn up at the sight of the cross or the taste of the sacrament on her lips?

She was mad that she had let Louise and Madeline's teasing get to her like this. She exited her mother's rooms and began looking for her companions ready to tell them off.

Frances finally came across them in the gardens. She was instantly annoyed that they had disappeared from her rooms. Weren't they supposed to wait on her? Their giggling stopped as she approached. It did not escape her notice that Madeline hid something in the pocket of her gown as she curtseyed to her.

"What is that in your pocket?"

Madeline stepped back nervously. "It's nothing. Just a trifle."

"Show me," Frances demanded, extending her hand.

She did as she was bid and beside her Louise shifted on her feet. Madeline placed an object cool to the touch in Frances's palm.

Frances examined the colored stone wrapped in red string. On one side a strange figure was engraved on it. She passed her finger over it. It almost looked like Greek letters though she did not recognize which one.

"What is this?"

"A charm."

Frances's eyebrow went up and without needing to be pressed more Madeline explained.

"It's a love charm. If I keep this with me until the end of the year I shall find my one true love."

Frances flinched. "Magic?" Dropping the object on the ground as if it had burned her. Madeline was quick to scoop it up and place it back in her pocket.

"It's just something we got from the market. Some old spinster was selling potions and charms."

She stepped forward to whisper so they wouldn't be overheard. "Some say she's a powerful witch."

"It is forbidden! You could get into a lot of trouble if you get caught."

"It's harmless. Besides the girls in the town say she is a good witch not the kind that gets burned at the stake. She goes to church." Madeline smirked. "I'm surprised you are so high and mighty given that your grandmother enchanted King Edward under an oak tree or so my mother says."

Frances bit the inside of her cheek.

"Those are lies. I shall tell my mother you are spreading slander about our family and then we shall see who is sorry."

Louise was tugging at Madeline's sleeve as if to stop her from engaging further in this.

"Well anyways," Frances regained control of her temper. "I am sure that woman is a charlatan, and I hope you know that you have wasted all your pocket money on a useless charm."

"Why don't you go see her for yourself? Who knows

maybe you might see some family resemblance." Madeline whispered this under her breath but Frances heard and clenched her fists.

"You are right. I shall go see her — to denounce her for what she is!"

~

Frances tried readjusting the ill-fitting dress for the umpteenth time.

"You are fine. Stop doing that or you'll draw attention to yourself."

"It itches too." Frances couldn't stop herself from complaining.

"Probably has fleas."

Frances bit back a cry but couldn't stop her hands from itching at the bodice some more.

The trio had snuck out into the busy streets of London — they had claimed they were giving alms to the poor after Mass but instead left to go to the market. The other girls seemed to know the way better than Frances, and, for once, she let them go ahead of her.

Madeline and Louise had helped each other change in the stables before helping Frances. They dressed in borrowed gowns from the maids.

They walked past what Frances could only describe as the Goldsmiths Street — shops lining the street advertised their wares in the large window panes. Signs hanging out of doors were decorated with names painted in gold lettering like "Edward's Fine Jewelry" and "Green's Gold".

When they turned on to the main street, she nearly took

a step back. Here the narrow streets were packed so tightly with people and noises that she struggled to keep up. Frances yearned to pinch her nose shut against the smells but thought better of it.

No one had time to look at three girls running about. Perhaps they were maids running an errand — it turned out it was not completely unusual.

Finally, reaching the docks where vendors from afar were displaying their wares on rough tables, they slowed their pace.

Louise took Frances's hand and led her towards an old woman manning a stall. No one was around her stall, but she didn't seem to mind. She had a toothpick clenched between a pair of thin cracked lips, and a red kerchief wrapped around her head, though grey wispy hair seemed to have escaped in most places.

When she saw the three of them approach she gave a toothy grin, and Frances saw that she had several missing teeth.

"Ah, I recognize you," she pointed to Madeline. "What can I do for you little misses?" Her gaze moved to the purses tied around their belts.

The way she stared at them made Frances wonder if she could see inside them and was counting the coins that could be hers.

"My friend here wanted to see you," Madeline pointed to her.

"Want a charm? For love?" the old woman asked, waving a hand over the baubles on display. Staring at Frances some more she added. "Or maybe one for beauty or luck?"

Frances frowned. "I need neither of those things."

"Perhaps something to help you with your enemies then? Would you like to send a little bad luck their way?"

"Are you a witch?" Frances blurted out the question. The woman's face fell and for a moment she got the distinct impression she had been tempted to leap out of her seat at her.

"No, of course not," she laughed. "I was a tinker's wife and now in my old age I have settled here in this great city."

"Then how do the charms work, if you do not have any magic?"

"I have faith," the woman turned serious again, beckoning her forward. "Like you do when you pray at the altar. God has given me gifts, but nothing I sell can do more than nudge fate one way or another."

"Such as finding love?"

"Yes, of course. Don't you little ladies pray for a handsome rich man to ask for your hand in marriage? These just helps to attract that sort of luck your way."

"But if this is Godly work — are you a nun? Why are you charging money for these... trinkets?"

The woman huffed, not too pleased at the interrogation. "Nothing is free in this world, girl. Do you think the priests pray for the souls of those in purgatory for free? Do you think they will bless you without a donation to the church?" She laughed a cackling sound. "No, of course they don't. I'd be a fool not to take money for my services. How would I eat? Anyways, since you don't want a charm. Perhaps you would like your fortune told?"

Frances gulped. This was surely something her mother's priest would disapprove of, but curiosity overtook her.

Madeline and Louise were nodding their encouragement too.

"Fine." She eyed the woman warily as she pulled out a worn looking chart.

"Sit down," she pushed out a stool for Frances with her leg and laughed when Frances tried to dust off the seat.

"A little dirt won't harm you," she focused on Frances as she began arranging the chart. "Do you know when you were born?"

"Middle of July."

"And how old are you?"

"Don't you know?"

The tinker's widow tutted to show her irritation.

Frances saw the woman study the chart her fingers moving along the grid lines to what she saw were star signs.

"Turn over your palm."

Frances complied, easily mystified by the woman now.

"Well?"

"So impatient. Much like your sign — cancer." Frances watched as the woman seemed to mull over her chart, glancing every now and then at the upturned palm on the table. After some time, she sighed and leaned back in her stool. "You are a fighter and you shall spend your life fighting."

Frances put her hand back in the folds of her gown. This wasn't a very promising start.

"I see a husband and children in your future but you shall have to face struggles as well," the woman intoned sagely. She went on about how Frances would live in the lap of luxury but face illness in her lifetime. Then finally, she suggested she might benefit from a bit of extra luck.

This shook Frances out of her reverie of the old woman.

"I don't think my parents would approve of such things."

The woman shrugged as if she didn't care, though she had slouched now, visibly disappointed she wouldn't make a sale.

"One shilling for the reading."

"But you barely said anything."

"The stars cannot divine everything in your future, and if I could see something more, then I might have people running around accusing me of being a witch." She gave Frances a pointed glare.

Frances fished out the coin from her purse and begrudgingly put it in the woman's outstretched hands.

"I don't believe you are anything but a charlatan."

"Believe what you will." The woman was more preoccupied with the coin than with her now.

Suddenly, Frances wanted to leave. The stench of the streets was making her stomach turn. She might very well get sick right now, proving the old woman correct.

"I will take a charm for luck." Louise pushed forward.

Once the sale was concluded Frances hurried the others home.

"Don't you want to stop and get some fresh bread? I have some extra c—" But Louise couldn't finish as Frances interrupted her.

"No — I want to go home and get out of these rags." She found the itching hard to ignore now. "We wasted so much time and money here. I hope no one has noticed we disappeared."

She walked in silence, rolling her eyes as the two of them compared charms.

There was nothing in that woman that Frances recognized. She doubted she was even a witch. It was more likely she was a gypsy swindling silly girls out of their money.

～

Frances was balancing on the heels of her feet as she was poked and prodded by the seamstress.

"Stop that," her mother chided. "She needs to get the proper length."

"Never fear, Duchess," the seamstress reassured her. "I'll leave a good amount of hem so it can be let out as the little lady grows. This shall be a brilliant gown."

Frances was in no doubt of that. Her mother was keen on dressing her in the best money could buy. The cream brocade overcoat had slits in the sleeves to reveal a plum red undershirt and the kirtle was also dyed the same shade of plum, embroidered with tiny white pearls.

Despite the richness of the gown, it was more uncomfortable and heavier than anything Frances had worn thus far.

This Yuletide, Frances was to accompany her parents and, much to her displeasure, her younger brother, to court. She often teased him that he had been ennobled as the Earl of Lincolnshire before he could even speak.

She had attended court before on special occasions, but now her mother had decided she could perform her duties well enough to be found a permanent position. It helped that she was mature for her age and that her dancing had improved somewhat. But Frances wasn't sure if she could manage any grace weighed down by this gown.

With the start of these celebrations, she would enter the Queen's household as a maid in waiting. An honor that she had waited for a long time.

Especially when it meant she would finally escape the nursery at Suffolk Place.

She was also eager to get away from her sister Eleanor. She was tired of being compared to the younger, wittier girl. Who at the age of eight was already fluent in three languages and amused their parents with songs on the lute.

By comparison, her own playing sounded like a child twanging the strings. Frances never missed the way her mother flinched at every wrong note. Her father always applauded politely but never asked for a repeat performance.

It left her feeling insignificant and outclassed, which she felt was unfair. She was the eldest — shouldn't she be the one to shine? She worried that her mother would have Eleanor join the Queen's court as well, but it seemed that decision would be delayed for a year or so.

Frances heard her mother and father discussing that it might be better to give her the chance to thrive at court without being upstaged.

This had hurt her feelings but there was nothing to be done. At the very least, her position as eldest in her family could not be taken away from her. If something — God forbid — happened to her brother she would be her father's primary heir. That made her important. And that was more important than succeeding at Latin or dazzling her parents with music.

She returned from her mother's solar with a grim look on her face. She had been left sulking on the unfairness of the lot she had been dealt for too long.

"What is wrong?" It was Eleanor who pounced on her first. "Did you not like your dress?"

"It was lovely. You shall probably never have anything as fine as it."

Eleanor did not seem to notice the scathing tone in her voice, but Louise and Madeline were much more attentive.

"I am sure she shall have a dress just as dazzling as your own."

Frances wanted to tell them to shut their mouths. "Soon I shall have my own rooms at court and I shall leave you all behind."

"I'll miss you." Eleanor seemed sincere and Frances patted her on the head.

"I shall visit in the summer. Of course, the Queen might wish me to accompany her while she goes on progress."

Madeline looked skeptical but by now knew better than to contradict her.

Frances ruled over the younger people of the house.

～

It was not long before her trunks were packed and belongings stored away. They were going to Greenwich. It was not a long journey from their London home, but Frances was still excited and kept asking if she should bring certain items with her.

"Can I bring Phillipe?" This was her little dog from the

Spanish Ambassador. He had traveled a long way to be with her.

"You can send for him after you have been settled." Her mother was craning her neck to see if the footmen were placing the trunks carefully on board their barge. This had been her mother's personal barge when she was still Princess of England. Now it was refitted to suit her new station as the Duchess of Suffolk. The Tudor banner was displayed proudly alongside the quarterly coat of arms her father had adapted.

"Will Father greet us?"

"No, we shall see him at dinner. We shall go straight to the Queen's rooms where you shall be formally introduced and made to swear fealty to her."

Frances nodded. She felt like she had asked this question several times, but she never grew bored of the answer. "Will there be many people there?"

Now Mary was growing impatient with her. "Most likely. Can't you just sit quietly?" Moments later, they set off in the decorated barge, with the sound of the drum setting the pace.

~

Frances followed after her mother — they did not stop, though her mother gave a nod here and there in greeting or acknowledging a bow with a quick dip of her own.

They moved through the Queen's familiar presence chamber and strode past the guards into the privy chamber beyond. There the Queen sat, surrounded by her ladies as she read a book of hymns. She looked up and smiled as she saw the pair of them.

"Ah, the Duchess of Suffolk has arrived. Sister, you are welcome to court!"

Frances watched her mother step forward to her old friend and give her a respectful curtsey before the two women embraced.

"You are well?" The Queen's Spanish accent was thick as she spoke.

"Yes, thank you, your highness."

The Queen motioned for someone to bring a seat beside her. "You shall sit beside me." Then her gaze went back to Frances.

She gulped as the Queen's attention turned to her and made her deep curtsey just as she had practiced in her bedroom the night before.

"Very pretty, you are becoming more like your mother every single day." Queen Catherine's compliment made her flush red. Though she doubted the truth of her words.

"Thank you for taking me into your household, your highness. I hope I shall serve you well."

"I do too, dearest niece. Come kiss my cheek and then you may take your place beside your mother."

Frances did as she was bid. The Queen's cheek was smooth but gaunt. As she sat, she noted the white strands of hair peppering the bronze from beneath her hood. It seemed Queen Catherine had aged in the last few months since she had seen her last.

As she settled on her stool, Frances looked about the room. She recognized several faces, but then her eyes settled on Mary Boleyn. She regarded the blonde woman with some jealousy — had she somehow become even prettier since the last time she had seen her?

She put this down to the pretty new gown she was wearing. It was much finer than what she had ever worn before.

A dark-haired woman sitting beside her seemed entranced by her own book. Turning to either her sister or the lady beside her to show them a passage. The lilting laugh of the woman was distracting.

Many couldn't help but turn to look her way.

Frances struggled to remember her name. She knew she was a Boleyn sister, but she had hardly bothered to make note of her name.

Her mother was whispering with the Queen so low that even she couldn't hear. So she took this time to look around the room. On previous occasions when she had been at court, the ladies had looked at Frances with jealousy, coveting the place she held near the Queen, but now they were more focused on the dark-haired woman.

Some regarded her with hatred while others seemed to glance her way with admiration.

Frances wasn't sure what to make of this and turned a distasteful glare towards the Boleyn women. They were messing with the order of precedence.

Later in the morning after they had all processed to Mass, a page boy announced with great fanfare that the King was on his way. He wished to spend some time with the Queen and her ladies before escorting them into dinner for the Feast of the Immaculate Conception.

He entered the Queen's privy chamber with a spring in

his step, hands on his hips he stood examining the women who had leapt to their feet to curtsey low to him.

Her sense of propriety couldn't stop her from sneaking a peak. The King was majestic in cloth of gold, a great chain hung around his broad shoulders. Jewels decorated his cap and the pins in his shirt were also shimmering as they caught the sunlight.

Behind him, his favorites came piling in. Frances spotted her father just behind the King.

"You may rise," he declared, and to his wife he stepped forward and bid her a good morning.

Frances thought the tone of voice was cold and disinterested.

"I hope you are well as well, my lord husband." There was a slight tremor at the word husband but she hid it behind a gracious smile.

"Welcome sister," he greeted Mary with the same brotherly affection he had always shown her. "I hope your journey was pleasant."

"It was, thank you, your grace," she returned his greeting with one of her sweetest smiles.

He turned around and called for music. "Why is it so quiet in here? It's not as though this was nunnery."

"I assure your majesty this is no nunnery," the dark-haired woman had dared to speak.

"Shall you entertain us with the lute, your grace?" Queen Catherine spoke loudly to Mary, preventing the dark-haired woman from speaking more.

"I shall be honored."

Frances watched her mother move to the center of the

great room. A groom had provided a stool and another lady brought forward a beautiful lute inlaid with gold.

Mary tested the strings and jumped right into a ballad. This was one her brother had composed the year before. This seemed to please him and he took the seat offered to him by Queen Catherine.

Her mother's skillful playing could not keep the King's attention for long. Even Frances could see how his eyes danced about the room but always returning to the dark-haired woman. At times Frances caught him looking at her with such intensity. His eyes seemed to darken and his mouth parted as if he would say something. He seemed desperate to be by her side and not the Queen's side.

It almost made Frances pity him.

Her mother and father were regarded as a great love match. They had married in secret without the King's permission and had not even waited for the customary year of mourning, for her previous husband the King of France, to pass. Yet Frances had never seen her father look at her mother that way. Nor had she seen her mother send such coy glances back at him.

Frowning, Frances turned to see what the Queen would do, but, if she noticed, she said nothing.

Later that night she asked her mother about the woman.

"That was Anne Boleyn. Don't pay her any attention — she is a low-born woman," Mary scoffed.

"The King pays attention to her."

Mary shook her head. "It is a trifle. We must serve the Queen and help her in this most trying time."

That seemed to be the end of the matter and Frances was about to go, but her mother grabbed her arm.

"Whatever you may hear, the Queen is the only Queen and we shall serve her faithfully."

"Of course!" Frances frowned. What else would she be?

∾

It did not take long for Frances to learn how wrong things were going for the Queen. Within a few months of her arrival at court, there was no longer any mystery surrounding the King's intentions. It was an open secret that no one dared talk about but everyone knew about. The King was questioning the validity of his marriage. His next choice in bride was clear too — he had his sights set on Anne.

After Christmas, she never seemed to leave his side. As a maid of honor who helped the Queen get ready for bed, Frances knew that the King had stopped visiting her bed.

Catherine staunchly refused to give any credence to the rumors and went on as usual. Behind the closed doors of her privy chambers she would sit at her little desk and write letters by the fire long into the night. Frances was by her side, ready to fetch her more ink, or sharpen her quill or refill her glass. After helping the Queen into bed, she would sleep on a palette set at the foot of her bed.

It was an honor she coveted and Frances made sure to perform every service with perfection.

∾

She was fetching the Queen's smelling salts that she had left in the chapel during Mass when she spotted the King walking with the Lady Anne Boleyn among the hedgerows.

Anne Boleyn was now absent from the Queen's rooms most of the time. She had been given her own apartments and had a group of ladies serving her as if she was someone of importance. This in particular made Frances resent her even more. She was spending her time alternating between serving her mother in her own apartments and the Queen — and she was the daughter of a Duke! Why should this work be beneath someone like Anne?

Frances paused to study them.

Anne was speaking to the King in a very animated fashion. She couldn't hear what was being said, but the King seemed absorbed in every word as though he was trying to commit them to memory. Then Anne placed her hand over his, almost as if she had done this by reflex. She gave a little gasp and seemed to blush, taking the hand away.

It left Frances with a strange feeling in the pit of her stomach to see the King fawn over Anne.

She wished she could be as fashionable and desirable as this woman.

No one ever talked of her beauty or wit. A few of the other girls would whisper about men who would ask them to dance or give them little gifts. Of course, nothing serious ever happened as Queen Catherine would be sure to dismiss them from her service if she heard of any untoward behavior, but it left Frances on the sideline.

Whenever she was asked if she found anyone attractive, she would turn up her nose at such questions and say she had no time for silly flirtations. Her family was arranging a brilliant marriage.

At night she would dream of being married off to a Duke or perhaps, like her mother, she would be sent off to France to marry a Prince.

"Why are you dawdling in the stairwell?" Maria de Salinas, Baroness Willoughby interrupted her thoughts.

Frances flinched at having been caught out. "I was fetching something for the Queen."

"Then you had better hurry." Maria had no kindness to show her. In her dark black gown of mourning she cut a severe figure. She had always been a joyous woman easy with her smiles, but recently she had become defensive and sour. Her expression fixated in a grimace.

It was no secret that after the death of her husband, she had become embroiled in legal battles with her brother-in-law over her daughter's inheritance. Frances had heard this from her mother and father on the rare occasion they shared a private meal in their apartments.

Without any further hesitation, Frances ran off but looked back to see Maria staring out the same window, her face set in a grimace at seeing the King below.

~

The beginning of Lent was upon them and a great banquet was planned to begin the celebrations on Shrove Tuesday.

Frances was excited for the chance to wear her magnificent gown again. She was helping her mother dress in her room, handing her jewels and pins as her lady-in-waiting asked for them.

"Have you practiced the steps?" her mother questioned.

"Yes, every night." Frances did not add that she had not managed to add any graceful flourishes to her movements.

"Good, there will be a lot of people watching and plenty of foreign ambassadors."

This made Frances's stomach clench in fear rather than encourage her.

"Your father wishes you to be personable," her mother added, examining the rings on her fingers and exchanging one ruby ring for another.

"I shall try." Frances's throat went dry. Now she was worried about saying the wrong thing and embarrassing herself.

She left shortly after as she had to get ready herself.

The ladies were using an antechamber off the main hall where the masque would be performed. She had been given a minor role at the request of the Queen.

Her aunt had meant this to be a treat for Frances, not understanding how terrified she was of performing before an audience.

Frances was stripped down to her petticoats by ladies and helped into the costume — a long sleeveless robe of white damask replaced her over-gown. The light fabric of the sleeves was fastened in place by broaches creating a draping effect near her shoulders. Next came tight white sleeves which were pinned in place before another layer of hanging sleeves were added. These sleeves were made of fine white gauze.

Her soft leather slippers were replaced for white ones and a mask was secured to her face with a white ribbon. Her hair was plaited and piled high on her head, with only a gold hair comb as a decoration. Frances felt exposed without a hood.

Around her, seven other ladies were being similarly dressed. They were a dazzling assembly of white.

She tried her hardest to ignore the eighth lady who was dressed in a similar costume but in gold rather than white. The costly cloth glittered and her red petticoat made her stand out all the more. On her head, her sister was carefully pinning a gold hood in place on her silky black hair. The hood had been altered. The veil was removed and all around white satin flowers were propped up to create a halo of dazzling white. In the center a large ruby drew the eye. Anne Boleyn wore it like a crown. She was certainly dressed as richly as any Queen.

The master of the revels soon called them all to attention and informed them to take their places in the main hall. For once, it was empty of all people except for the few putting the final touches on the décor.

In the center of the room stood a fountain, a hawthorn tree and a mulberry tree. Frances took her place with the other ladies on the bench while Anne Boleyn stood before them. To her right, a painted screen decorated with red roses hid a small choir from the Chapel Royal.

Frances spotted a small boy hiding in the alcove, biting his lower lip. He was dressed up as Cupid, in a white doublet and hose, a set of gold wings attached to his back and carrying a fake bow and arrow.

Time seemed to stretch forever as they waited for the court to arrive.

Frances found herself fidgeting with her girdle until Lady Hastings next to her told her to stop. She tried controlling her breathing but this did nothing to stop her heart from racing. Instead, she took to praying that this ordeal would be over with soon.

As if answering her prayers, a fanfare of trumpets down the hall announced the King approaching.

Everyone became serious, straightening their backs. The choir master began directing the first of many hymns so when the King finally entered, accompanied by ambassadors from France and Spain on either side, they were greeted by a beautiful display and soothing music.

Anne Boleyn had turned her back to the crowd awaiting the beginning of the dance. Frances hoped she saw the disdain on her face and that it would make her falter and miss her steps, but, as always, Anne seemed impervious.

Perhaps she was used to hatred from women just as much as she was used to love from the men. The thought made Frances smug.

As soon as the rest of the court were seated and the Queen had taken a seat on the raised dais, the Lord of Misrule appeared before them. In a booming voice that echoed through the hall he announced the start of the masque.

The choir began singing the lyrics to a song composed by the King himself. It spoke of the beautiful goddess Venus watching her son Cupid playing in the garden.

At this point the little boy came leaping from the alcove, spinning and twirling around the fountain. Venus turned to face the crowd, and strung her harp as her child played. The crowd murmured appreciatively, much to Frances's dismay.

She tried to maintain the smile on her face but found

herself slipping. They remained on the bench for quite some time.

The boy made a small speech about the beauty of love. Then a man strode into the hall waving a wooden sword. He was dressed in grey and declared that he would make sure that Cupid would be unable to spread the joy of love to anyone.

At this point Frances and the rest of the women made a great show of gasping and looking afraid. Venus, still playing the lute, sung a pretty song imploring someone to come rescue her and her son from such a vicious attack.

In response, a blare of trumpets sounded and in came the god Mars, behind him marched eight soldiers. Mars challenged the grey man to a duel, and they made a fine show of sword play before finally the man in grey fell to his knees in defeat.

Venus came forth and bowed to Mars thanking him for his bravery and courage.

At this point, music from the rafters filled the room and the pair clasped hands to begin the dance. The other men invited the ladies in white to dance as well and Frances took the hand of Sir Francis Bryant and let him lead her around the fountain and elderberry tree.

Then the pairs danced around Venus and Mars.

Frances was counting the steps in her head, her concentration must have been so obvious that Sir Bryant gave her a reassuring smile which made her all the more embarrassed. She nearly tripped as they spun around but he managed to keep her upright and Frances hoped no one had noticed.

As the song drew to a close, they all dropped to their knees in a synchronized bow, heads down to the floor as

Venus declared that love triumphed over all as she remained in Mars's arms. Cupid danced around the pair throwing white rose petals in the air.

Finally, to the applause of the court, they stood and unmasked each other.

There at the center was Anne and the King flushed from their dance and beaming at each other. The reveal came as no surprise to anyone, but still they applauded even louder and sung the King's praises.

Frances looked to the Queen to see what she would make of this obvious show of love and favoritism. Queen Catherine did not miss a beat — she was on her feet applauding with the rest so as her husband looked out at the crowd he saw her. She stepped down from the dais and curtseyed before him.

"That was beautifully done, my lord," she said, a hand to her heart as if she was left breathless herself.

He smiled in response.

The Queen turned around, the swish of her gown swatting Anne's. "Shall we not have another dance?" she asked the court.

Shouts of agreement filled the hall.

She turned back to her husband. "Shall you dance for us again?"

The King nodded, motioning to the musicians to start up another song.

In one stroke, Catherine had shown Anne that she did not see her as a threat, and, by giving permission, she was in essence giving her ascent to her being in the King's favor. Frances grinned, for she could tell that Anne, whose smile was now finally faltering, was very much displeased. She was reminded that she was not Queen.

Bryant took up her hand again, leading her to join the others dancing and Frances had to focus on her steps yet again.

After one last song, they departed, pulled by a chariot out of the hall.

Back in the antechamber, she changed back into her original gown of cream damask with the plum kirtle. She desperately wished to keep the beautiful sleeves of her costume though they were quite indecent. A maid helped tuck her hair into a coif cap and then adjusted her French hood ensuring she was every bit the proper lady again.

When she finally joined the rest of the court her mother pulled her aside.

"You didn't do so badly," she said as she adjusted the pendant of her necklace. "Tonight, you shall sit with your father and myself."

"But shouldn't I be seated with the other ladies?" Frances would much rather sit with them than worry about every movement she made being scrutinized by her mother.

At her mother's raised eyebrow, she looked down.

"Come along and for Heaven's sake remember to smile."

Frances let herself be dragged away. She did her best to fix her features in a pleasant smile.

Her father had an honored place near the King's own table. He was one of the leading men in the realm and one of the highest ranking as well.

She picked at the food placed before her, finding she had no appetite for the rich food served tonight. This would be her last chance to eat eggs, meats and cheeses but she found they made her sick to her stomach.

Men and women came and went from their table stopping to greet her mother and father, sometimes whispering news or asking for it in return. Frances was thankfully ignored.

The French ambassador came up to them, sweeping a special bow to her mother.

"France is not the same without you, my lady," he winked. Her father laughed at the flattery.

"But she blooms ever so nicely in England does she not?"

The ambassador nodded in agreement.

"This is your daughter is it not?" He turned his gaze to Frances. She did not enjoy being scrutinized, but she did not look away either.

"Yes, it was time she joined the court."

"Perhaps you would honor me with a dance later on?" He gave her mother a little bow when she nodded her assent.

"Excellent." He clapped his hands together and then turned to her father and the two talked about other things not concerning Frances or her mother.

"Don't embarrass me," her mother repeated as they sat back down.

Frances wasn't sure how she could reassure her mother that she never sought to embarrass herself or anyone but sometimes things were beyond her control.

As the banqueting dragged on, Frances was invited to dance several times by her mother who encouraged her to partner with a variety of people. She suspected that her mother was trying to show her off to the court, but she was not the favorite lady that night.

As she sat in her bed that night, she felt dismayed that she had failed to make much of an impression. It made her sulky even the following day when even the Queen noticed her sallow face.

"What is it, Frances?" The Queen invited her to sit beside her before Mass.

She couldn't bring herself to tell this great lady the truth. After all, Catherine had greater problems and made a better show of strength than she did.

So instead she settled for a half-truth.

"I want to be like you and my mother. You have such grace and strength and I fear I shall never be like you."

Catherine was perhaps shocked by her candid response for she was silent for a few moments.

"We all have our own strengths. You are young and shall come into your own. I have no doubt of that. You have royal blood running through your veins and the blessing of God. Turn to Him and He shall reward you." She took Frances's hand in her own. "Nor should you compare yourself to others. God has set you in your place and given you many gifts. You should not question them, but thank Him for his many blessings. I was one of many sisters, and yet I knew that despite my shortcomings I was destined for great things and that my parents loved me dearly. Jealousy is a sin."

Frances swallowed hard. What the Queen said struck a chord deeply within her.

"Thank you, your grace." She found herself wiping a stray tear away from her eyes. "I shall strive to improve myself and learn to be grateful and truly worthy of the position I was born into."

"I am glad." The Queen released her hand and returned to her reading.

～

The season of Lent ended quickly with the swift arrival of early summer heat bringing the cool wet spring to an abrupt end. This spelt the beginning of a troublesome summer for Frances. The heat coincided with outbreaks of the sweating sickness. The doctors predicted this would be an unusually rough season as there seemed no end to the heat.

As soon as an outbreak was reported in London the King retreated to Greenwich, which was farthest from the city, and then from there fled into the countryside. Her aunt, Catherine, went with him. Despite their recent travails, he had not abandoned her.

Many of the court were left behind, however, Frances among them. She returned to Westhorpe Hall in the country with her mother while her father accompanied the King.

In her own element, she took to ruling the nursery once more. She pretended like she was too old to play games with the others in the school room. She had left such things behind and had become a lady. But of course, most days she found herself wandering into Eleanor's rooms.

She took on the role of instructor from time to time, correcting her manners and pointing out her mistakes. She left Eleanor in tears once.

"How shall I ever go to court?" she wailed. "I cannot do anything right."

"You are still young." Frances was not very sympathetic. She was secretly pleased that her sister was not overly confident and full of herself. "I don't think Mother and Father will have you come to court for a few years."

"Oh good." Eleanor looked obviously relieved.

Just then, their mother appeared. Behind her trailed a girl Frances vaguely recognized.

"Frances, Eleanor, I have someone to introduce you to." Mary motioned to the mousy brown-haired girl at her side. "This is Katherine Willoughby, your father's new ward. She shall join our household."

Frances looked from her mother to the new girl. She was about her age, she was still dressed in black for mourning and looked dour. Didn't she know how lucky she was for the opportunity to join such a well-connected household?

"Make sure she is welcome. I have to speak with the lord chamberlain about dinner." With that, Mary left them alone.

Eleanor looked curiously at the newcomer, but her childish shyness waited for Frances to say something first.

"I know your mother, Maria de Salinas."

"You do? Have you seen her recently?" Her eyes went wide and she looked as though she was holding her breath for news.

"No, I have not seen her since May. She is traveling with the Queen, but you shall see her when we return to court in the fall," Frances said, though she couldn't be sure her mother would be willing to take her with them.

At this Katherine beamed. Frances had not been looking to cheer her, up but she seemed easy to please. She was also happy to see that Katherine did not have any notions of grandeur.

In the next few days, she was looking up to Frances and deferring to her in a way that her own sister never did. Frances, who had her doubts at first, equally warmed up to her.

∾

"Are you feeling alright?" Katherine pulled up beside her on her grey hunter.

Immediately, Frances straightened in the saddle.

"Yes, of course. I was just giving my horse time to rest. Maybe he threw a shoe."

Katherine probably did not believe her, knowing by now that Frances had a fear of jumping with horses, but she would not embarrass her friend by pointing this out.

"Shall we turn back?"

Frances twisted her head around. The chimneys of Westhorpe Hall were still visible.

They had ridden out alone, promising not to go past the river. This was all her father's land and she could ride through it without worrying about being waylaid by bandits or robbers. Her father's men patrolled regularly and kept the peace. No one dared cause trouble on the Duke of Suffolk's land.

"No, let us continue. I — this horse should obey me better." She dug her heels into the horse's side. It pawed the ground ready to shoot forward but she kept a firm grip on the reins.

"Don't do that. The horse is probably nervous and it senses your disapproval." Frances looked at Katherine to see if she was being patronizing, but, as always, she looked innocent. "My old master of horse taught me to look straight ahead when taking a jump and lean forward. It will encourage the horse and you won't be tempted to pull back on the reins. If the horse is nervous, this showing your own bravery will help."

Frances frowned. "I know how to ride a horse."

"I'm just trying to help you. I've ridden many difficult horses," Katherine said with a shrug. "My father used to say I was wild."

Reminded that Katherine's father had died, Frances felt pity for her. "Alright, I'll try it your way. Since you are the expert."

Katherine merely smiled at the scoffing tone she used.

She managed to jump over the log in their way and they continued riding through the forest. Her mother had not let them go hunting today, so they wandered aimlessly.

Frances set her face in a grim determination as she pushed her horse onwards taking more and more dangerous trails. Her mother had been surprised by her recent interest in riding and hunting, but Frances had determined she would become a great horsewoman. She just had to get over her fear.

She remembered how everyone at court said Anne Boleyn was a fabulous rider and was only beaten by the King. It had become fashionable for ladies to take to the saddle and every ambitious father encouraged their daughters to ride out whenever the chance arose.

Frances was not about to be left behind.

She had been surprised by the easy friendship that had cemented between Katherine and herself, despite the two-year age gap between them. She was tall and mature for her age, so it felt more like talking to a peer than her younger sister.

More than that, Katherine did not brag or seem overly gifted. Perhaps she did not have a competitive bone in her body. Frances put this down to her less than illustrious heritage. While she was one of the wealthiest heiresses in the land, her mother was merely a Spanish gentlewoman and her father had been a count. It was nothing compared to Frances's family tree.

She knew from her mother that her father planned to have Katherine betrothed to her brother Henry once he was a bit older. She was lucky to be allowed to join their royal family.

∽

The summer passed by quickly. Her mother was busy tending to the estate, although in times like this she mainly stuck to overseeing the house being cleaned and kept free of disease. She also ordered poultices to be made to help stave off the sweating sickness.

Tenants came to her bearing bad news of failing crops, and she had watched her mother rail in frustration. Their family was powerful and should technically be wealthy, but every quarter they had to pay out a heavy fine to the King. This was their punishment for their secret wedding.

Frances did not understand why the King didn't just pardon their debt to the crown. He always said Mary was his favorite sister and Charles was his best friend.

Rumors reached them that Anne Boleyn had fallen sick with the fever. The King had sent his own physician to tend to her but had obviously not gone himself. Her mother seemed smug and reassured that any day now they would hear news that Anne had tragically passed away and that the King would drop his quest to divorce the Queen.

It seemed such a certainty that Frances began daydreaming of returning to court and becoming the favorite. With this in mind, she practiced dancing and playing the lute every moment she got with Katherine, who was only happy to comply.

At length, she found herself improving. Her mother was also too distracted to come and watch her with the dance master so she was spared her criticism.

With the return of cooler weather, sickness seemed to abate. There were no new reports of illness and the household seemed to breathe a sigh of relief. This season they had been spared.

A neighboring town had not been so lucky and on their ride back into London, they rode around the town to avoid catching any lingering sickness that might be lying in wait.

Frances felt confident and strong enough that she did not ride in the litter with her mother but rather on a horse of her own. Katherine rode at her side talking pleasantly of her childhood in Lincolnshire.

As they rode through London, some in the streets called out blessings to their party.

"God Bless, the Duchess of Suffolk!" an old woman called down.

"À Tudor," a man doffed his cap.

"The pretty Princess!" another called.

Frances watched her mother wave to the crowd and occasionally throw coins to the poor children dressed in rags. Thus, their procession to Suffolk Place was slowed. Frances tried mimicking her mother, standing up straight in the saddle and looking important. In the past, whenever they had processed from church or through the streets she had always hidden herself away.

The gates of Suffolk Place swung open to admit them.

Her mother was helped down from the litter by the lord chamberlain who was already pressing her with questions.

"I shall look into it later," Frances heard her mother's exasperated response.

A groom helped her jump down from the saddle even though she could manage on her own just as well.

Beside her, Katherine looked glum, which baffled Frances. Suffolk Place was as grand as any residence in the Kingdom. Its chimneys towered over other buildings and there was a pretty view of the Thames and a small park to walk in.

"Come along, I'll show you to my room. You can sleep with me and keep me company. It's the best room in the house." She meant this to be a special treat for Katherine, but she had only managed a nod.

Her room was indeed furnished very finely. It was not as big as her parents' rooms, of course, but it had a window overlooking the river. On warmer days, a pleasant breeze would roll in too. The big four poster bed was piled with blankets, pillows and coverings.

She had her own little prie-dieu which had a real gold cross on the shelf before a beautiful altarpiece — painted by the monks. She showed her little treasures to Katherine who remained resolutely silent.

"What is wrong with you?" Frances finally couldn't hold herself back.

"I am sorry. I just remember coming to London with my mother and father. We don't even have our London house anymore. My uncle is claiming it as his own inheritance and until the matter is resolved we cannot go."

Frances was taken aback. She was suddenly mollified. Of course, she must be reminded of her old home. She had not thought of this.

"Suffolk Place is my favorite. You shall grow to love it even more than your own house. Besides, my father is fighting for your father's will to be followed, so you shall have it back."

Katherine nodded and the girls shared a smile.

"Let's go. I'll show you around. We have a wonderful library here." It was fashionable to own books and be very learned. For her part, Frances liked sitting in the library, but she rarely ever had the patience to read the tomes her father collected. She usually brought her needlework inside or relaxed on a chair in there.

～

After three days of running around Suffolk Place and buying trinkets at the market, the royal barge arrived to escort them to court.

"The King sent this just for us," Frances bragged to Katherine who was impressed by the rich trappings. She had not yet traveled in the royal barge herself.

They stepped on the gangplank and took their seats. They did not sit under the canopy of estate, for, though they were of the royal family, they had no right to it.

Once her mother's maids had stepped on board too, the rowers pushed off. The barge glided steadily down the river.

The trio found the Queen's rooms were strangely silent and felt almost empty. They bowed deeply to the Queen, and Katherine greeted her mother for the first time in months.

Frances did not concern herself with her but rather focused on the Queen and her mother talking quietly, heads bowed together. The Queen was talking rapidly, and her mother seemed shocked by every word that came out of her mouth. She moved closer to them but Mary gave her a look that told her she was not welcomed.

Instead, Frances took a seat beside the Princess Mary who had come to visit. She was a year older than herself but she was still much shorter. At the moment, she had a pale pallor that was unflattering against the dark gown.

They kissed and greeted each other as cousins, though Frances bowed low to the heir of the English throne.

"How is it at Ludlow?"

This was the wrong question to ask for the Princess's face scrunched up, which Frances thought looked even more unflattering.

"I am glad to be here with my mother and father," she eventually replied.

"What are you working on?"

"A shirt for my father." She handed it to Frances, who examined the fine black thread stitched into the collar.

"It is very fine work. How do you manage it?" Frances thought of her own needlework work that looked clumsy compared to this.

"I spent years practicing and my mother taught me. I can show you as well," Princess Mary offered.

Frances spent the morning by her side practicing on scraps of cloth, all the while watching the Queen and her mother who had gone visibly pale.

"Where is Anne Boleyn?"

Frances had looked around the room and had not seen any of the Boleyns or Howards.

"They do not attend my mother, but it is just as well," she replied, snapping a piece of thread. "God shall surely punish such sinful behavior."

"Tell me, what has happened?"

Princess Mary leaned forward and spoke in a low voice. "She has been heard saying that she would rather see all the Spaniards dead at the bottom of the sea than serve them again."

"No!" Frances gasped. "Has she been banished from court?"

Princess Mary shook her head.

"What? But..."

"She retains my father's favor."

Frances wondered if Princess Mary knew that he

wished to marry Anne Boleyn and put her mother aside. Tactfully, she did not mention this to her.

That night, instead of sleeping in the Queen's rooms, she was sent away to her mother's rooms so she was witness to the loud argument her parents were having.

She entered the privy chamber and could hear them shouting from their bedroom. Frances sent away her maid so she would not overhear as well. She didn't even have to press her ear to the door to make out what they were saying.

"He cannot do this!" her mother shouted.

"He is the King!"

"I shall speak to him."

"I forbid it!"

Something smashed against the floor.

"You cannot stop me."

Her mother came flying out of the bedroom and came to a halt when she saw Frances standing there.

"What are you doing here? Go to your rooms," she snapped.

Frances thought it was unfair she was taking out her anger on her, but she did as she was bid.

∾

The next day Frances was summoned from the Queen's to her parents' rooms. Frances had been sitting with Princess Mary and looked at the groomsman confused.

"What has happened?"

"You are to come away at once, I am sorry, my lady, I don't know more."

"If they have summoned you, then you have no choice but to obey," Princess Mary encouraged her.

Not one to be shown up or wanting Princess Mary to think she was not Godly and obedient to her parents, she stood up as imperiously as she could manage.

"Very well." She bowed to the Queen who gave her a small smile, and then bowed to the Princess before leaving.

Her mother was red with rage, ordering the servants to hurry up packing their things. Her father was slumped in his chair. Frances saw they were making an effort not to look at each other.

"Mother?"

She swung around. "There you are, get your things packed, we are leaving."

"What?" Frances took a step back. "But I am a maid in waiting to the Queen. She relies on me. I cannot—"

"Did you not hear me? Do I have to have you whipped until your hearing improves?"

Frances gasped. "N-no, of course not. I am sorry." Her mother's threat silenced her and she ran from the room.

It was not until they were floating down the Thames that she dared speak again.

With an eye on her silent father brooding on the prow of the barge, she sat beside her mother bundled in furs against a chilly autumn breeze.

"Lady mother, why have we packed away our things? Is something wrong?" Her voice cracking as she spoke.

"We have been banished from court."

Frances fell back and had to grab on to the arms of her mother's chair to keep from falling to the ground.

"What do you mean?" She was shaking.

"We are going to Suffolk Place and then to Westhorpe Hall. What can't you understand?" Her mother's voice was cutting. It no longer held the sweet softness she was famous for.

Her mother's eyes were fixed on the horizon.

"But I was to be betrothed... I was going to serve the Queen. How can I go? I have done nothing wrong! What did you do?" Frances knew she was babbling but she could not comprehend why they had left in such haste. Why had her life been suddenly turned upside down?

Her mother's slap sent her crumpling to the floor. She lay there in a sobbing heap until the barge was docked.

It was her maid who urged her to get up. Frances did not wish to go. She wanted to command the rowers to take her back to Greenwich and the court. She wanted to show them how well she could dance and ride now. She wanted to be a great success.

Finally, it was Katherine Willoughby who managed to get her to leave the barge.

"They lit a nice warm fire in your room, and I asked them to bring you a hot bath. You'd like that wouldn't you?"

Frances wiped her tear-stained face, noticing how the skirts of her gown were also wet with her tears.

"We will change your gown and you can go rest. We aren't leaving for another day or so until they pack up the house." The younger girl placed a comforting hand on Frances's shoulder.

It struck Frances that she was making a fool of herself, allowing Katherine to take charge of her.

"I shall go to my room," she declared, standing up.

They walked up to the house, much to the relief of the rowers who had waited for her to depart.

"I am sorry we have been taken away from court," Katherine said.

Frances wanted to lash out at her. What did it matter to her if they left? Wasn't she already betrothed to her brother Henry, the Earl of Lincolnshire? Wasn't it a brilliant match? Once her brother was old enough they would be married and she would become a countess.

The thought of Katherine outranking her irked Frances. She couldn't imagine walking behind Katherine and giving her deference. She didn't even want to think that one day, her father might die and her brother would become the Duke of Suffolk. That would make Katherine a duchess.

Meanwhile, she was left with nothing. No betrothal. No inheritance. No position at court. Wasn't she worthier than the younger Katherine? Wasn't she born to the royal family?

"Do you think I can send a letter to my mother?"

This drew a stop to her inner ranting. Of course, Katherine would be missing her mother. Frances's pity was invoked for her again.

"Of course, you shall! And if anyone says anything they can come talk to me," she said. "I am sure this has all been a misunderstanding and we shall be back at court in no time. At the very least we shall go to court by Christmas."

~

Of course, they did not return. Frances had been shocked to learn they had been banished from court. Her father had told her after she had pestered him. He was still not speaking to her mother, and Frances knew then that it had all been her fault. She had done something to upset the King.

Her father had assured her that they would return to the King's good graces, but in the meantime, they would go to Suffolk.

Her mother did not appreciate the silent reprieve she was receiving from her husband. It was Frances and Eleanor who bore the brunt of her fury. Frances was actually happy when they reached Westhorpe Hall, so her mother might find some other release for her anger.

Slowly, Frances pieced together the story of what had really happened. Her mother had gone to the King and protested that he should not seek to put the Queen aside and disinherit his daughter. Her mother was always close to Queen Catherine and had been horrified to learn how far the matter had gone.

More than that, her mother could not bear to think that her friend would be displaced for a commoner like Anne Boleyn.

She reminded her brother — quite rudely — that he had once defended the sanctity of marriage, pressing their sister Margaret to stop seeking a divorce from her second husband. The King, who had always treasured his younger sister, recovered quickly from the shock of her impudence and told her to hold her tongue or he would have her sent away.

Mary Tudor, who had always been petted and favored, thought she might call his bluff. She had not realized how serious he was. The famous Tudor temper came out and here they all were now.

Frances understood her mother was correct. The King should not seek to annul his marriage just because Queen Catherine had not been able to give him a son. It was God's will after all. But he was claiming that their marriage was a sham for she must have lied about being a virgin when they married and that is why they remain without an heir.

She thought Princess Mary was the heir but, apparently, she did not count. Frances wondered what the Princess thought about that.

Her mother spent her time hunting in the forest while her father heard petitions from the local lords and gentry. They lived separate lives for a long time but slowly things began to mend.

Frances was sitting with her mother in her solar, the large windows overlooking the green park when her father's groomsman came in carrying a small gift for her mother.

Mary opened the box and saw a little jewel inside. She sighed happily and told the groomsman to tell her husband that she was very grateful.

"He wished me to ask if you will eat in the great hall today, my lady?"

"Yes, I shall," her mother handed the gift to her lady-in-waiting to tuck away in her jewelry box.

By the end of October, they were fast friends again.

Frances asked her mother on a weekly basis if she might return to court, and, when Mary received a letter from Queen Catherine, she would ask if the Queen had summoned her.

"No, of course not," her mother frowned.

"Well, what does she say?"

Mary threw her a look that said she was testing her

patience.

"What news from court is there?" Frances tried again in a sweeter tone.

"The King planning to summon a parliament to discuss the validity of the marriage." Her mother seemed apprehensive.

"But surely, there is no grounds." Frances thought of the wise Queen who was so fastidious in her faith she might be a saint. Was not having a son grounds for divorce?

"Wolsey might find some ground. He is a miracle worker."

"But he's the Cardinal! He will take the Queen's side. Everyone knows she is right."

Mary regarded her for moment making Frances wonder if she had said something foolish.

"That might not matter," she sighed. "The Cardinal has always done whatever the King asked of him. So the King will have his way and they will find a way to persuade the Pope. I fear that woman may be leading him into sin."

"Anne Boleyn?"

Her mother nodded. "She will not find it easy taking the Queen's place. I pray she never succeeds."

"I pray that also," Frances said.

Later that day she told Katherine the news. "It is not right for a man to put aside his wife just like that."

"I can't imagine it," Katherine agreed. She looked horrified, her mother was closer to the Queen than anyone else, and she had been named after her.

"What's worse is if that low-born woman sits on her throne!" Frances continued. "I swear I shall never curtsey to her. I shall never talk to her."

Katherine gave her a wry smile as if to say she remembered just a few months ago when Frances was seeking to copy Anne.

The cold weather brought a bout of sickness down on her mother. The shock of banishment had been too great and she took to her bed. Frances stayed by her side as a good daughter should and prayed for her mother's recovery day and night.

She confessed to their priest that she had been angry at her mother and prayed to be forgiven.

Her father sent for physicians and wrote to the King. At length, he sent one of his own doctors to look at Mary and see if any treatment might help her.

Frances looked away as her mother was leeched. She couldn't stand the sight of those wriggling creatures. She was also prescribed a course of poultices to drink, which smelled so bad and must have tasted even worse for it made her mother vomit more often than not.

It took her mother a month to recover and her recovery coincided with the beginning of the Yuletide celebrations.

Frances was upset that her mother had not seemed to be grateful to her for staying by her side. She felt she was downright indifferent to her. She tried talking about this with Katherine but Katherine had not understood.

"It was your duty to stay by your mother's side," she had said, frowning at Frances. "Why should she treat you any different?"

"You don't understand," Frances was frustrated. She could have been practicing dancing or sitting idly in her rooms. Didn't Katherine know that she didn't have to sit by her mother's sickbed? Of course, as the loyal daughter that she was, she had been more than happy to serve her mother.

But she deserved some acknowledgement for this service. After all, hadn't her mother taken her away from court and her prospects?

"God shall reward you," Katherine said piously.

Frances could say nothing else but agree with the sentiment.

In the end, it was her father who decided she was to accompany him to court. He was given news that he was allowed to appear at Christmas and beg forgiveness of the King. Mary was still not invited back.

Frances doubted her mother was ready to apologize anyways. Her parents still had terrible rows about this. Her father always urging her to write to the King with her apologies, something her mother staunchly refused to do. She was sure he would summon her back eventually.

"Shall I have a new gown?" Frances asked hopefully, thinking back to last Christmas.

"No, but you may wear one of my old ones." Mary called for a maid.

"Bring up my green satin gown, with the rose embroidery," she commanded and the maid left to go to fetch the dress.

Once it arrived, Frances was helped into it but found it tight around her chest and shoulders.

"It shall have to be let out and hemmed." Her mother looked displeased. "What have you been eating? At this rate you will be a stout pony instead of a delicate rose. You must get this from your father for all the women in my family have been dainty."

Frances bit back a retort that Queen Margaret, her aunt in Scotland, was not that dainty either. She was happy to leave her brooding mother behind as she traveled with her father and Katherine as her companion.

~

The Lord of Misrule ran around declaring that he would bake his wayward dog into a pie if he didn't return his wooden scepter.

Katherine was laughing heartily but Frances couldn't bear to enjoy herself today. The King was missing from his chair underneath the cloth of estate. Still servants brought dishes to his table and presented it to the empty chair before presenting it to the Queen.

Frances could see she was not eating anything even though she made a show of heaping food on her plate.

She, like everyone else at court, knew where the King was tonight. Publicly, he was dining at Bridewell, but in truth he was with that woman at Suffolk Place.

Her father's penance had been extracted by the King. He was to be his friend and whole-hearted supporter again. So now that woman slept in their best rooms and traipsed around their great hall as though she owned it. It made Frances sick to think of her enjoying the luxuries that had been meant for their family.

She said as much to her father who responded by threatening to have her whipped if she made her feelings known. Even so, Frances knew that her father disagreed with the divorce. She had heard him wishing that the King would drop this matter or that Queen Catherine would agree to enter a nunnery.

Much to everyone's dismay, none of this occurred yet.

Frances looked from the Queen to Cardinal Campeggio dining beside Cardinal Wolsey. They looked tired and just as worn out by this trial as the rest of the court.

Catherine of Aragon had proved to be a worthy adversary for some of the smartest men in the world. She had argued her case with the help of Bishop Fisher and had left the King and the Cardinals chasing their tails. But could Catherine really win?

Was Anne Boleyn really worth all this trouble?

Frances bit the inside of her cheek. To think just weeks ago she had been worried about getting herself back at court.

She had known that the King was trying to set his wife aside, but she had not thought he would go ahead with it. Her mother had always been so adamant that this was just another of his passing fancies that he would quickly grow tired of Anne.

She was wrong. They all were and now they were sitting here playing along to the King's charade. The King who always loved masking was busy playing the part of the loving husband for the papal legate.

Frances, who was back in the Queen's rooms, knew this was a farce. He never came to spend time alone with her or even to share her bed. He only performed before a crowd. This perhaps hurt Catherine more than anything else. At night, Frances would hear her dry sobs from her truckle bed at the foot of the Queen's bed.

Catherine never smiled any more, and she yearned to

see her daughter. Princess Mary was being kept away from court. She had not been invited to join the celebrations. The official excuse was to spare her the stress from the ongoing trials, but really the King was trying to find ways to punish Catherine and force her hand.

On multiple occasions, the King told her she could go but that if she left, she wasn't welcome back, so she stayed.

A choir came to sing a beautiful hymn and a professional team of maskers performed, but they received a lackluster response from the court or even the commoners outside who feasted on the leftovers of their betters.

When Queen Catherine stood, everyone did the same and bowed low to her as she left the great hall and the yule log burning brightly. Many would disperse but many others would hang back to dance and discuss matters further.

Frances didn't quite understand why this matter had become such a topic of conversation. Everyone was taking sides but besides the tragedy to her family, she didn't see the significance of the King's decision to divorce his wife.

She was lost in her thoughts so she yelped when Anne Hastings dug her elbow into her side.

"What?" She scowled with indignation.

"The Queen has called for you." She paused. "Twice now."

Frances felt her cheeks burn red, and she ran into her aunt's private study, her gown swishing behind her.

"Ah, there you are, Frances." Catherine regarded her from her writing desk. "Come here, I would have you do something for me."

Sensing she was about to be given an important task, she rushed forward and knelt by her side.

"I would be honored to serve you."

Catherine placed a cool hand on her cheek. "Shall I have you sworn to secrecy?"

"I would never betray you."

"I was teasing you. You have grown serious since returning to court." The Queen removed her hand and Frances saw she had a far off look on her face. "I know you would never betray me but neither does this task require much secrecy. Though your silence would be appreciated.

"Please go summon Mendoza to come see me tonight. Have him come in private and as swiftly as he can."

"I shall go." Frances rose to her feet, straightening her gown about her.

Catherine looked amused at her show of vanity and Frances flushed red. What did appearances matter when your whole marriage was being questioned?

She left the room and, making some excuse to the ladies in the privy chamber, she headed towards the great hall. She wasn't sure who to ask about how to find the Spanish ambassador, but she thought she might try there first.

No one paid much attention to her and she walked among the tables looking around all the while for the dark-haired man. She was in luck as she spotted a man with the double headed eagle of the Holy Roman Emperor on his livery.

"Sir, do you know where Ambassador Mendoza is?" She stopped him in his tracks.

He seemed taken aback by her question, and he looked ready to leave when she squared her shoulders and stood up straighter.

"I need to speak to your master, immediately. I have a

message for him."

Perhaps it was her haughty tone that did the trick or the fact that he couldn't see the harm in it, but, at length, he shrugged and nodded, leading her out the great hall. The ambassador was given rooms on the first floor of the palace. Far from the King's rooms and very inconvenient. This was meant as an obvious slap in the face to him and to Spain.

The man knocked at the door and was admitted inside, Frances standing in the doorway. She watched him approach his master, muttering to him in Spanish. Mendoza turned to her, his gaze critical until he finally recognized her.

"Lady Brandon." He swept her a polite bow.

Frances curtseyed in response before nodding.

"Will you come inside?" He motioned to a chair by the fire.

She shook her head. It might be seen as improper.

"I have a message from the Queen." She glanced at the manservant, wondering if he was trustworthy. "For your ears alone."

Mendoza grew serious now, and he dismissed the man with a smile before approaching her. This was the first time Frances was this close to Mendoza, and she realized, unlike other powerful men like her father, he was neither tall nor broad-shouldered.

"She asks you come to her rooms tonight. In secret if you can manage it," she whispered.

"What for?" Mendoza had a conspiratorial air about him.

Frances did not know, but she did not want to let on

that she was not privy to the Queen's council.

"I cannot say now." She looked over her shoulder. "I should go before I am missed. Can you come?"

"Yes, of course. Tell her to expect me before nine."

Frances gave him a curt and serious nod. "Very well."

She caught him trying to stop from smiling. Perhaps she looked silly trying to play the serious lady. Straightening her back yet again, Frances marched away from his rooms — proud that she would be sleeping in the Queen's own chambers tonight and not in the worst rooms in the palace.

Mendoza appeared as promised, and he sequestered himself with the Queen and Lady Willoughby in her study.

Frances kept watch outside the doors. She tried to look inconspicuous stringing a lute, but she knew the other ladies could guess the Queen was plotting something behind closed doors. At least they would not be able to hear.

The Queen did not speak to her until she was in her bed, and Frances was extinguishing the last remaining candles.

"Come here." The command was whispered so low that Frances had barely heard it.

"What is it, your grace?" She approached the older woman who, under the covers, did not look like the imposing Queen that she was.

"Take this." She stretched out her hand. A small rolled up letter was in her hands.

Frances did not hesitate to take it.

"It is a letter for my daughter." The Queen let out a sigh. "I fear that woman has convinced his majesty to keep her from receiving my messages."

"What am I to do?"

"Keep it safe and give it to your mother once you leave court. She will see that it reaches Princess Mary." Catherine grasped her hands. "Swear to me on this crucifix, that you shall not tell anyone and keep the letter safe."

Frances felt the sharp stones of the crucifix dig into her palm. "I swear."

"You are a good girl." Catherine released her hands.

The rest of the Yuletide celebrations passed by quickly, yet Frances felt as though something was always caught in her throat. She had done as her aunt asked and kept the letter secret, but she worried it would be discovered or that she was doing something wrong. Especially if the King was forbidding the Queen from sending letters.

After Christmas Day, which was celebrated with two masses and punctuated by a feast that lasted well into the night, her father announced they would be returning home.

"To Suffolk Place?" Frances was worried she would have to put up with serving Anne.

"No, to Westhorpe Hall."

The journey was slow, as the snow had left the roads hard to cross. Frances was wrapped in furs, yet she still shivered and wished her father had thought to bring a litter with them. She wondered if this was God's punishment for carrying the secret letter.

Her mother was happy at the sight of it, though and she asked for news. Frances managed to disappoint her in this as well, since she had nothing to tell that Mary did not already know.

"Who dined with the Lady?" her mother asked.

"I do not know. Many of the court disappeared with the King. The Queen was quite bereft."

"Never mind, I'll ask your father."

"He says we are to support the divorce."

Frances looked away from her mother's piercing gaze.

"Of course we are." She paused. "Go away, little fool, and play with your friends."

"I am not a fool," Frances muttered under her breath so low that her mother couldn't hear it over the sound of her heels as she strode out of her rooms.

Katherine was more sympathetic to her.

"My mother just doesn't understand," Frances was telling her. "We cannot displease the King or we won't be allowed back at court."

"But if he does something that is wrong... or against the will of God..."

Frances considered this throughout the day.

That evening she questioned her mother. "How can my uncle be wrong? He is the King. It is the lady who is cruel in separating the Queen from the Princess."

Her mother looked as though she would argue but thought it wasn't worth her time.

"You'll understand one day."

CHAPTER THREE

1529-1530

HER MOTHER WAS STILL NOT INVITED BACK to court. The continued punishment made Mary short-tempered. At the same time, she doubled down on her belief that she was right and, therefore, was suffering like any other martyr. It was through her father and visitors that they received any news.

The Pope was not being swayed to side with the King. As the continued guest of Emperor Charles, the Queen's nephew, he was hardly about to declare against her.

The King's growing frustration by the Pope's continued delays and Campeggio's stalling left people afraid of what he might do.

"She's given him books to read," Charles confided to his wife.

Frances, who was sitting with her mother, gazed up

from her sewing and looked with interest between her parents.

"So?" Mary seemed uninterested but Frances knew her father wouldn't have mentioned it unless it was important.

"Some might call them heretical but the King finds them intriguing."

"Why?"

"They agree with his logic."

"Of course they do! Why would she let him get his hands on anything that doesn't make him seem to be in the right?"

"Bishop Fisher is fighting for the Queen. He and other men are to stand as her legal representatives and advisors."

"They dare?" Mary gasped.

"Yes, braver men than me." Frances saw her father's shoulders slump in defeat.

There was silence after that. Mary had made her feelings known multiple times. But they had already faced the King's wrath a few times and had paid a heavy price. They would leave the debating to the religious men of the realm.

〜

"My mother has written to me." Katherine had run up to her wide eyed and pensive.

Frances gave her friend her full attention.

"She says the King has decided to go ahead with the trial and that we should pray for the Queen."

"She dared to write this to you?" Frances snatched the letter out of her hands.

Katherine shrugged. "Everyone knows she is my mother's dearest friend. Even if she did not write to me everyone knows her thoughts already."

"Alright, well it's a nice day, perhaps we can go riding today."

"The dance master is coming in the afternoon to teach us a new dance," Katherine reminded her.

"What does it matter if we never return to court?"

"We will."

Sometimes Katherine's blind faith surprised her but also cowed Frances, for she was reminded of her own imperfect faith.

"I think I shall go to the chapel and pray as my mother bids me to do."

"My mother will accuse you of becoming a nun," Frances warned.

"You are joking!" Katherine was frowning. In her mother's household, piety had been encouraged and there was no such thing as showing too much outward faith.

"Not at all. You know how she is. A lady must be entertaining and ready to laugh. She often says I am a lost cause. After all, I have neither trait and no beauty either."

"You are healthy and strong — and pretty when you smile."

Frances scoffed, a hand went up to the mark on her shoulder. "But not as beautiful as the women of my family."

"You act as though beauty is the only thing that matters in life."

"Only for those who aren't beautiful. No one will write poetry to me or pass my love tokens." Frances was entering one of her self-pitying moods. She thought of Eleanor, who grew prettier by the day. She was fair and delicate — just like their mother. Frances had to confess weekly to the sin of jealousy.

"That would be improper. It is better to live a life of virtue."

Frances rolled her eyes. Her friend could be so worldly and serious sometimes. "It's nothing but courtly love."

She stood. "Well, let's say a prayer for the Queen and then go riding," she compromised, pulling Katherine along.

∽

Parliament was not disbanded that summer, much to the ire of the lords who could not leave the stifling city for their cool country estates. Frances had begged her father to accompany him to court to witness the trial. He was in a dark mood and refused.

At length her mother also insisted she go.

"And take Katherine Willoughby with you, she can keep Frances company."

At this point, he knew he couldn't argue.

"You might be able to attend the trial as well. If you just wrote to your brother."

"I already wrote to him but I will not... I cannot support what he asks of me."

"Take care not to anger him further."

"I am not a fool." Frances did not miss the way her mother gazed her way at that.

∽

Court had moved from Westminster to the more modern Bridewells Palace. It was conveniently connected to Black-friars where the trial would take place.

The city was abuzz with gossip. Most were supportive of the Queen, but they did not place any bets on her winning. With the trial, the city also saw an influx of people. If her father wasn't a favorite of the King, he wouldn't have had a place to sleep at court.

Frances found herself walking into the Queen's rooms at Baynard's Castle with Katherine following at her heel. The younger girl was intimidated by the clergy and great men of the realm present. Not wanting to show her own discomfort, Frances walked with purpose and did not gape at the rooms which had turned into a study.

Among all these scholars was the Queen, dressed in a harsh black gown. It was still richly embroidered with silver thread and her fingers were heavily jeweled with many rings.

They received the briefest of acknowledgements as they entered. Frances sat among the other ladies, asking Anne Hastings when the trial would actually take place.

"Not for another week now." Anne Hastings bit her lip. "Can you imagine what she must be feeling? Poor lady."

Frances looked to her aunt, but she did not see a poor woman. She saw a woman who had decided to stand up for her rights and take the brave step of defying her husband openly.

For two days they endured a miserable existence. There was no fun to be had at court. No one danced in the evenings, no one played bowls in the gardens or took out a deck of cards. As if sensing it would be inappropriate, no one dared call for music.

Then, in the upper chamber of the castle, the Queen made a formal appeal to Rome.

Frances watched from the sidelines as her aunt proclaimed that she could not get a full trial here in England and wished the Pope to take the trial of her marriage on himself. He would be her judge and no other. This she swore before two notaries and several clerks who recorded every word.

After this, she retired to her bedchamber. Here, she was no longer the strong woman but looked every bit like a woman who had aged before her time. Her face seemed more lined than ever. She slumped in her chair, and, though they placed heavy blankets on her, she still shivered.

"He will be angry with me," she whispered this as Frances began removing her headdress.

She didn't have to say who, nor did Frances have any words of comfort for her. Yes, Frances could imagine his anger, and, for that very reason, she had taken to pretending she was elsewhere.

Soon, this trial would be done and the court would return to its old ways of merrymaking.

∽

At last, the King opened Parliament. The Parliament Chamber for the trial had been meticulously prepared. Frances had seen for herself the pages of the wardrobe running back and forth, carrying heavy cloth, cushions and hangings. It was lucky for them that the storehouse was so close.

On the day of her trial, the Queen had awoken early, bathed in a steaming hot bath and was dressed with meticulous care by the most senior of her ladies.

Frances watched each item being draped over her aunt. Each layer was another layer of armor, each jewel a weapon. She looked every bit the royal Queen that she was.

In her head, she went over what would happen today.

They would process into the court as part of a great retinue of lords and ladies. No less than four bishops were to enter with the Queen and several leading theologians. Frances had not seen much of her father leading up to the trial, but she knew he would be there. Her mother had told her she wished to know everything that was happening and so Frances tried to memorize every little detail.

Finally, it was time and Catherine seemed to have turned to stone as she led the procession to the court. They arranged themselves by order of precedence, the bishops walking immediately behind the Queen, then the lords and ladies.

Frances jockeyed for position. She was the daughter of a duke and had royal blood in her veins. She procured a spot for Katherine as well. She needed her friend by her side.

As they entered, it was clear that the councilors and judges were shocked by the Queen's personal appearance. Frances looked to the empty throne on the right and saw that the King had sent a proxy rather than come himself.

Instead of taking her seat on the smaller throne on the left, she approached the judges sitting frozen in their seats. Cardinal Wolsey seemed exasperated.

Bishop Fisher handed her a piece of paper, which Frances recognized as the written proclamation she had made earlier protesting that the Cardinals did not have the jurisdiction to judge the validity of her marriage. This was something she left for Pope Clement.

Campeggio and Wolsey conferred with each other. It did not take them long to reach a response. They decided to delay yet again.

"We shall consider your protestation and respond in kind, in three days," Wolsey spoke. From the way he fidgeted in his seat, it was clear he was trying very hard to keep his frustration at bay.

"Very well, my lords," Catherine bowed.

They all processed back out again. Frances wondered what this had all been for, but it seemed the Queen had won herself something precious — time.

"That wasn't so bad," Katherine whispered to her as they walked back to the Queen's rooms in a much less formal manner.

"That was just the first day," Frances said knowingly. "My father says it shall last several days if not weeks."

"Oh."

∼

The next time they went to court, things were much more formal. The King had attended himself. He was sitting in his throne under the cloth of estate. The Queen took her own seat and Frances along with the other ladies retreated to the back of the room, past the clerks and the members of parliament standing judge. Once everyone appeared to have settled down and take their appointed spots, the court crier called for silence.

Frances struggled to see what was being done and said. But she knew that the King had been called, for he stood up from his throne and called out "Here, my lords!"

He said a few words. Something along the lines of the fact he only questioned his marriage for the benefit of the realm. The Cardinals then also spoke in turn.

Frances frowned. No mention was made of Anne Boleyn, but was she not the reason behind these proceedings?

Then the crier called for the Queen. All eyes zeroed in on her. What she did next shocked Frances.

In a loud clear voice that even she could hear in the back, she denounced the Cardinals, appealing once more to Rome. To Henry, she had few words to say, but they were cutting.

"It seems your soul has burdened for a very long time, my lord. If there ever was a time for you to speak, now — after twenty years of marriage — was not the time."

This had enraged Henry as she knew it must have. He rebuked her arguments.

"Are you not the Queen of England? Are you not safe here? You appeal to Rome but you know perfectly well of the influence your nephew has there," he all but spat. Frances flinched from his rage though he was far away. "I would desire nothing more than for our marriage to be declared valid."

Following this, the Queen stepped down from the dais.

Frances thought she was leaving the court, but, instead, she went around the court and barriers set up and knelt before the King. She could not see her aunt any more but could picture her prostrating herself before her beloved husband.

The voice that carried across the hall was cracking under the weight of the emotion with which she spoke.

"I beseech you..." she began. The rest was lost to Frances as she was pushed further back by the crowd.

At length the Queen rose up, but, instead of returning to her seat, she proceeded out of the Parliament Chamber.

Frances tried to push her way to her.

The court crier was demanding her return, but the Queen paid him no attention. She did not falter. Frances turned to the King who was urging the court crier to summon her back. His face was red with fury.

Applause was heard as the Queen walked past the common people who had packed in to watch the proceedings.

Frances slept in the maid's chambers that night so she could gather as much gossip as she could. She could hardly question the Queen herself on what had been said.

It was Mary Norris who had all the news.

"He gave her permission to appeal to Rome."

"No, he didn't," another girl contradicted her.

"Not in so many words no, but he might as well have." Mary Norris shrugged.

"He said he loved her and wished for their marriage to be declared valid, so why wouldn't he agree to appeal to Rome." Frances agreed with her.

"Why do this at all then?" Lucy Talbot was confused.

Frances wanted to roll her eyes. "Because..."

She was cut off by Mary Norris who always thought she

was so clever. "He wants to set her aside, if the marriage is indeed invalid. The King must have an heir. A male heir. Everyone says the Queen is too old now."

Frances rewarded her daring with a pinch. "You cannot say such things. It's disloyal to the Queen."

After this daring escapade of the Queen's, her father had her and Katherine sent for. They arrived at his rooms to find him instructing his master of horse to arrange for an escort.

"Are we leaving father?" Frances asked, curtseying to him.

"You shall be," he nodded to the man to go about his business before turning to her. "It would be better if you returned to your mother's side for now."

"But why?"

He looked exasperated but was nice enough to humor her rather than forcing her to obey blindly. "The Queen will not appear in court anymore, and, after her stunt today, I would rather you aren't seen in her rooms serving her all the time. The King is furious. I would rather avoid bringing down his wrath on our heads. Understood?"

"Yes, Father." Frances looked away.

She didn't quite understand but all these politics were beyond her.

~

Westhorpe Hall was stifling. There was nowhere to go for privacy as people filled the corridors seeking an audience with the Duchess.

Frances took to riding in the shaded forests whenever

she could get away. Katherine following along obediently. On rare occasions, Eleanor joined them too, though Frances made sure to let her sister know she wasn't welcome.

Her mother was reaching the end of her patience. She had become as nervous and anxious as a colt. The Tudor stubborn streak was still refusing to let her back down. It didn't help that her father was pressuring her to make further amends with the King.

When news reached them that the King had banished his wife from court and declared Wolsey a traitor, she finally relented.

The trial had indeed been adjourned to Rome, but that spelled disaster for the Queen and many others. The King was now threatening to break with Rome completely.

Frances knew her father was now truly wavering in his secret support of the Queen. Why couldn't she have just taken the veil and helped to resolve this matter quickly?

~

In early November, their whole great household set out to travel to London. Even her brother Henry joined them from his estates where he was ruling his Earldom through the help of his father's advisors.

She took this opportunity to tease Katherine about her future husband.

"He's such a child," she sniggered.

"He will grow." Katherine had seemed unconcerned.

"Well, I wouldn't put up with being engaged to a child. I hope now my father will arrange a brilliant match for me."

Frances was not as certain of this as she had been in

years prior. On top of this, she knew her father and mother were distracted by other matters. In her heart, she doubted they thought much of her lately.

They traveled to Greenwich but found that the King was set to depart to his new home of York Place. Her father told them that the King had taken possession of all of Wolsey's estates and property. He looked pointedly at her mother as if to say "See what happens?"

Mary Tudor tried to look unperturbed, but it stiffened her resolve to get in the King's good graces again.

They traveled to York Place on horseback, which made their journey less pleasant than if they had taken a barge, but, at length, they reached the renovated gatehouse.

The splendor of the residence was evident immediately from the stone workmanship decorating the exterior. Frances spotted Wolsey's crest etched strikingly over the key stone. The four leopards seemed to stare at them as they passed underneath. The lion in the center struck a pose, while above two birds perched and finally a Rose on top of it all — a nod to his royal master.

She wondered how long this crest would stay in place. Surely, the King wished to erase all memory of his bad advisor. Everything seemed strangely new. From the chapel garden, to the storehouses and the extensions obviously still in progress.

She followed her mother — her father was there to greet them and grooms were waiting to help them down from their horses. Already servants were rushing to unpack the carts of goods that accompanied them.

She watched her mother greet her father with as much warmth as she could muster. She kept looking around, expecting to be attacked. Her father took her hand in his and gave it a gentle squeeze to reassure her. He smiled over her head to Frances who curtseyed to him.

Their little makeshift family was reunited and walked into the Palace together. They would go to greet the King in a show of formal solidarity. Anne Boleyn was more than likely to be at his side, and her mother would have to bow to her and acknowledge her presence.

Frances had seen her mother rage just the night before at the thought of kneeling to her.

The King was in the great presence hall, as fine as could be found in any of his own palaces. In fact, it was more richly decorated than even Greenwich. The Cardinal's expensive tapestries and cloth was covering the walls, his candles burning brightly.

Frances turned away from her uncle to the woman sitting on his right. The place the Queen usually occupied. But now the dark-haired woman had seated herself there. She was not sitting on a throne or under the cloth of estate, but, from her dress and manner, it was clear she was a mere moment away from doing so.

"The Duke of Suffolk and Dowager Queen of France," the court crier announced as they entered.

Her parents bowed and then after a moment's hesitation Mary also greeted Anne Boleyn. Frances smiled, watching her mother give her the shallowest of curtseys that she could manage. After all, it was true she significantly outranked Anne.

If Anne was insulted she hid it very well.

Next, her brother went and greeted them. There was no hesitation on his part and he bowed low to both the King and Anne. Then again, he wasn't aware of the political fighting that was ongoing. Finally, it was their turn and Frances lead the trio, Eleanor and Katherine following just a step behind her.

The King was smiling at them and wished them well.

Anne had looked upon them as though they were innocent babes. Did she not know that Frances had served Queen Catherine herself?

Unfortunately, she did not see much more of the King that day as he quickly sequestered himself away with his advisors. Among his favorites were her father the Duke of Suffolk, the Duke of Norfolk Anne's uncle, and the newly made Lord Rochford, Anne's father.

Her mother used the excuse of watching the servants unpacking to avoid joining Anne in her rooms, which had become the center of this new court. She didn't have this excuse for long, though. By the afternoon, she decided she would have to make an appearance in Anne's rooms.

She acted as if this was a great sacrifice on her part, and it was with a heavy heart that she marched herself over there. Frances entered behind her mother, who seemed to study every detail of the room from the embroidered cushions to the carpets laid out on the floor.

Frances saw many of the Queen's younger ladies in waiting had switched alliances. Jane Rochford, Mary Boleyn and several other familiar faces were there. They seemed to gloat in the favor the King had shown them.

The ladies muttered to each other when Mary Tudor made her appearance. She did not ask for a chair from Anne but directed a groom to bring one in for her, and sat directly across from Anne and her ladies. A small show of defiance.

Her mother was too proud to ask a lady lower than herself for anything. She would not be beholden to someone like Anne.

In the end, Frances sat near her mother and Katherine situated herself behind her, not wanting to draw attention to herself. Frances was not invited to talk and just watched with growing apprehension as some sort of normalcy developed.

Katherine looked sullen and remained quiet the entire time. No doubt she felt she was betraying Queen Catherine and her mother's love for her.

"I wish we could go back and stay at Suffolk Place instead," she whispered to Frances who was forced to agree with her.

That night at dinner they were seated at the high table. Anne was once again at the King's side.

There was dancing after they ate, and Frances, who had been itching all this time to dance, found that she could not bring herself to do so. Unlike Queen Catherine's court, the ladies here were more openly flirtatious and daring. They danced a quick jig and she had no hopes of keeping up. She decided it would be best to strike up an image on trying to maintain her propriety.

Dancing was beneath her.

Her mother danced with her father, showing off her gracefulness. Despite her age, she was still one of the most beautiful women in the room. Frances knew she was hoping to show up Anne, who was neither plump nor fair like her.

With her cheeks flushing red from the dancing, she curtseyed to her brother who applauded and complimented her.

"Dearest sister, you have been missed from court," he called to her. "I hope you shall not leave it any time soon."

"No, your grace." She curtseyed again, sparing a glance to Anne at his side to see her reaction.

Anne was stony faced but quickly smiled and looked to Henry with one of her coquettish grins. She whispered something to him and he led her on to the dance floor.

Frances watched her flawless movements. It was true she was a very accomplished dancer. Her eyes seemed to light up with a passion as the music carried her away. She had neither the prettiness of her mother nor the youth of some of the younger girls in her train, but she entranced the room. The King was surely taken with her and for the first time Frances could see why.

Frances spotted the new Spanish ambassador Chapuys hanging back — a frown of displeasure on his face, but still even his eyes followed Anne's every movement.

Cardinal Wolsey had also disappeared from the King's rooms. It was now Bishop Gardiner who was the King's most trusted advisor and secretary. Sir Thomas More had also been elevated to Wolsey's old position of Lord Chancellor. He did not seem especially pleased by this and was talking to Chapuys quietly.

From what Frances knew of him, he was more a scholar than a politician. He was adamant about ridding England of all heretics. The way he spoke, one might assume the country was crawling with them.

Frances found this laughable, but she would never admit this out loud.

That first night proved to be the first of very long nights for her family.

In December, preparations were being made for the investiture of Thomas Boleyn to the Earldom of Wiltshire. This would be the first official royal ceremonies held in the exiled Cardinal's old home.

"Mother, shall I wear the cream and purple dress?" Frances asked her hopefully. It suited her complexion quite well and her mother had not allowed her to wear it for quite some time, not wanting to ruin the expensive dress.

"I suppose you may." Mary regarded her for a moment. "You may need to have the seamstress let out the hem. I think you have grown."

Frances puffed out her chest proudly. She was growing into a woman. No longer would she be considered a child. Soon she might be married as well and be given even more precedence than before.

And if a commoner could marry a King, why couldn't she have a King of her own? She thought the Dauphin of France might do. She heard he was handsome, or perhaps a Spanish prince, though that was unlikely seeing how England and Spain had become enemies.

It shocked the court to find Anne had been given a seat as though she was a royal consort beside the King at this event. Frances had seen her sitting by his side many times, but to sit in what looked like Catherine's throne was an abomination.

The rest of the courtiers seemed to think the same — those who weren't of Anne's affinity anyways. They looked at the Boleyns with spite, not only for usurping the order of the world but also achieving more than they could dream of.

It didn't help that Thomas Boleyn was also made Privy Seal, the third ranking office in the country mere days later.

But just like her mother, they dared not voice their opinions.

The Queen, somewhere in her rooms, was left practically abandoned and unwanted. It was clear the King was proceeding ahead with his plans without any consideration of her feelings.

~

"Hurry up, Katherine!" Frances called behind her while still urging her horse forward. She didn't want to get left behind in the hunting party.

They were riding through Windsor Forest, the hounds baying ahead as they closed in on their quarry.

Frances was irked by Katherine's slowness but didn't want to be left alone either. She did not have any friends among Anne's other ladies. It made her feel better to have someone at her side.

She could see the King and Anne riding ahead, the gold sparkling in the sunlight that streamed through the forest canopy.

Her mother had been ill again and did not join the court on its progress around the countryside but rather retreated to Westhorpe Hall. Her father had been keen for Frances to stay with the court and continue her education as a great lady of the realm.

It also lent some credibility that he approved of Anne with the King.

Mary had been unable to make a convincing effort so it

rested with Frances to keep the way smooth. Anne had a power over the King that was unexpected by everyone. He didn't want to find out what would happen if they crossed her.

Katherine's horse stumbled and she nearly fell off.

"Katherine!" Frances pulled on her reins, bringing the horse to a stop.

"I'm alright. I think my horse lost its shoe," she was panting as she tried to catch her breath. "I don't think I can go on."

Frances hesitated. She looked over her shoulder and saw the hunting party had nearly disappeared. She would be hard pressed to catch up now.

"It's fine let's turn back."

She turned her horse around and they trod slowly back to the stables.

"I'm sorry," Katherine said, but Frances was hard pressed to say anything to her. She couldn't help but resent the fact that she had failed to make any impression on the hunt today, and she blamed this on Katherine.

∽

This summer had been an endless stream of hunting excursions during the day and revelries in the evening. Following the return of Anne's father from France, however, the court set off for Surrey.

The new tilt yard at Hampton Court was complete, and Henry wished to make use for it. As it turned out, there was another reason. Henry summoned key members of his parliament.

Frances saw firsthand her father's mounting anxiety. He seemed to know what this parliament would be about, though he failed to share it with Frances.

A few days spent in the company of Anne and her ladies made it abundantly clear that the King was seeking a reformation. Anne often spoke about the corruptness in the church. Sometimes she even wondered aloud where in the bible was there any mention of a Pope.

Frances found this quite heretical. She was by no means a devoted woman but had been taught by teachers and priests how to read Latin and fear the wrath of God like any good Christian woman.

Her father seemed to believe that the King would not go so far as to break with Rome, but Frances wondered if he had already practically banished his blameless wife why not also ignore the Pope's ruling?

One thing she knew was that she would try to stay out of Anne's line of sight. She didn't want that dangerous woman to hold anything against her. It terrified her how much power she could exert over the King. At this very moment, Cardinal Wolsey was heading for the Tower accused of treason. He was sure to perish there.

~

Christmas was full of tension at court. The King and Queen would walk to Mass together as courtly custom still dictated. This was one of the few times Frances had seen the Queen. Her father had forbidden her to spend much time in her company though, she did sneak away to give her a comforting letter from her mother.

However, this Christmas, Frances was witness to Anne's conniving plots. Anne had already demanded the King to refuse to let Catherine continue sewing his shirts and had hired a woman to take care of his needs as, apparently, she lacked the talent herself. Now she was no longer okay with merely celebrating the holidays in her own court. She wished to be front and center.

She had not gotten her wish, but the King was ill disposed to Catherine nonetheless, as he saw her as the cause of his arguing with Anne.

They were sitting down to break their fast after Mass, when Frances saw Catherine itching to say something. She kept looking towards her husband then looking away.

"I shall go on the Thames after and I shall see you for the feast tonight, madam," the King informed her in a light tone.

"In the company of that woman no doubt?"

"What do you mean?" She should have taken warning from his icy stare not to proceed but she did not relent.

"That woman, Anne Boleyn. The fact you keep her under your roof is shameful. You hurt me personally by openly showing her favor and you are setting a scandalous example."

"And what is shameful about me spending time with an accomplished young woman?" He took on her challenge in calm silence, which Frances knew meant he had something up his sleeve.

"You alone know of the sin you are committing. Against me and God," the Queen was self-righteous in her tone.

"Madam, let me reassure you that though I spend time

87

in the company of Anne Boleyn, I have not done anything that you could call sinful with her."

She opened her mouth to argue but he continued.

"Indeed, I wish to spend more time with her to get to know her better. Seeing as I have set my mind on marrying her."

Catherine seemed stunned into silence. She regarded him just as coolly as he regarded her.

"I am still your wife, and until the Pope says otherwise, you are not free to marry."

"We shall see."

They were dining in semi-privacy with only a handful of lords and ladies present, but, by the afternoon, this conversation was repeated throughout the court. Everyone from the lowest scullery maid to the Bishop knew that the King had sworn out loud to marry the Boleyn woman.

Frances could see Catherine's hold on her throne was slipping.

～

"Did he really say that to the King?" Katherine asked in a horrified whisper.

They were strolling through the gardens. The walkway had been cleared of snow and the warm day had left Frances in need of some fresh air.

Frances had just been told by her father that he felt guilt was weighing on his conscience. The King was going down the wrong path, and, though he did not wish to argue with him, the rightness of the Queen persuaded him to speak out.

"I was there when the King questioned my father on what the Queen had said." Frances kept her friend on edge. "First, he had said the Queen would listen and obey her husband, the King, but she could not put his desires before two other things."

"What?"

"God and herself or something like that." Frances frowned. "Anyways, the King was furious. I think he realized even my father is against this divorce.

"The King wants her to retract her appeal to Rome."

"So he can try the marriage here in England again? Did it not fail last time?" Katherine was sharper about politics than she was sometimes.

"I suppose so. Maybe, he is surer of his advisors and lawyers."

CHAPTER FOUR

1531-1533

Ever since her father had declared for the Queen, it seemed as though nothing had gone quite right for them. Of course, the King still favored his friend, but he often chose the company of Anne Boleyn and her affinity. Thus, her father missed out on a number of posts that could have been awarded to himself.

More than that, it meant her father was too distracted to make any sort of marriage arrangements for her yet again. Frances often worried about being left a spinster while her parents were so busy with other matters.

Her mother had returned to court, but she rarely dared to visit the Queen. However, her quiet disapproval of her brother's behavior seemed to temporize the King from mistreating his wife too much.

Then the King decided to move the court to Hampton

Court. He rode ahead with Anne Boleyn as usual. The Queen behind them in her litter.

A few days after their arrival, the Queen noticed something wrong. Chapuys had been denied an audience with the King, who seemed to disappear for days at a time. This was not something new but what was new was the command for her to remain behind.

Frances was with her when Chapuys entered her privy room looking worried.

"The King has still not seen me," he began. "Nor has he given a reason why you are to remain behind while he traverses the countryside with that whore."

"It is not a surprise. He has put her at his side even on formal occasions now. He wishes to forget about me, but he will find that, while he can continue to diminish me, I shall not go anywhere." Her voice broke as she struggled to voice her beliefs.

Frances stepped forward, taking her aunt's hand in hers, trying to find some way to comfort her.

"I am afraid he shall act against you soon," Chapuys went on.

"I shall pray."

"I wish you could find some way to reconcile with your husband."

Catherine fixed Chapuys with a glare that said: *do you think that is not my dearest wish.*

He looked embarrassed and began anew. "I shall inform your nephew of the new developments here. I am sure he shall help your majesty in any way he can."

"Thank you," Catherine said dismissively.

Frances sat with her for a while after this. Wondering if

she should write a letter to her father as well. What was she to do if the Queen was indeed banished from court? Should she remain at her side?

She looked to her aging aunt. There was no future for her here. She knew she would have to abandon her — she might not have a choice in any case.

$$\sim$$

"I am to go to Windsor." Catherine's hands were shaking as she read the letter.

"And the King?" Frances asked.

"He is to go elsewhere..." Catherine paused. "He is banishing me from his side."

"You can refuse." Frances was sure she could.

"I am his wife. I must obey him."

"I shall write to him." The Queen did not spare her a second glance.

She rushed to her desk and dipped her quill in the ink. Frances watched helplessly as the Queen scrawled a farewell to her husband, wishing him well on his journey.

A messenger left immediately to deliver the Queen's letter. Catherine watched for his return from her window. When she saw the dust kicked up by the horse she bit her lip.

Frances knew she was saying a silent prayer.

The messenger entered looking abashed and embarrassed. He took off his cap and would not meet the Queen's eyes.

"What did the King say?" she asked. "Does he have some message for me?"

"He said he had nothing to say to you," he said. "Forgive me, your grace. He has written to the council."

"And?"

He shrugged. "I was not asked to carry the letter."

Catherine looked as though she was about to yell at him, but she restrained herself. Taking in a slow deep breath she dismissed him.

"Thank you for your service to me. You may go."

After he left, Frances turned to her aunt. "Should you not have sworn him to secrecy?"

"There would be no point. Besides, he gave the King my message in public, so by now I am sure half of London knows he has rebuked me."

~

It was her mother who brought them news of what the King had written to the council. She entered the Queen's rooms under the pretense of showing the Queen plans for a new masque, but, in reality, they sat together whispering secrets.

Frances was allowed to join them.

"He said many things in that letter. Mainly repeating that you were not his true wife. But the worst of it is that he himself did not call you Queen."

Frances could not contain her gasp and her mother glared her way.

"This is that woman's doing." Catherine shook with rage or perhaps grief at this latest betrayal.

Mary sighed. "Whoever's fault it is, you must be careful. Will the Pope not speak on your behalf?"

"I pray for him to do so daily. My lawyers and my

nephew work for me tirelessly. I know the Pope has said the King cannot remarry until he has reached a decision but he is also delaying."

Mary reached into the pocket of her gown and pulled out a small folded up piece of paper.

"This is from the Duchess of Norfolk." She placed it in her friends quivering hands. "May it bring you some sort of comfort."

Frances caught Jane Rochford entering and gave a cough to bring this to their attention. Catherine quickly closed her hand over the note and tried to mask her concern.

Mary spoke louder now, "And I shall ask the master of robes if we can have the red satin cloth for the costumes."

"Do that." The Queen played along.

Frances saw Jane smiling towards them with a knowing expression. That little spy.

She always seemed to be in and out of the Queen's rooms just as often as she was by Anne's side as her sister-in-law. Frances wasn't sure what she was playing at, but she knew Anne barely tolerated her too. Though she was sure she would never turn away information.

~

Princess Mary was just as inconsolable as her mother over these latest developments. She confided in Frances one day that she had thought the matter would be settled once the trial had been stopped and the appeal sent to Rome.

"I know the ten commandments say to obey one's parents, but I cannot help but think that my father is committing some grievous error."

They were walking by the Thames, enjoying the cool breeze on this hot day.

Frances nodded. "I don't like what is happening either. My mother is very distraught and my father... well..."

"He must serve the King. I understand."

"But should we not obey the King? The Pope has not spoken out on behalf of your mother. Could he not be correct?" Frances could not stop these treacherous thoughts, but she remembered how amicable the King had been at the beginning of this whole endeavor. He had been willing to pay the Queen anything if she agreed to annul their marriage.

Princess Mary stopped in her tracks.

"The Pope will speak for my mother. He fears alienating my father who has been threatening to break with Rome." She crossed herself at this. "I do not believe he could do that. It would be blasphemy as wrong as that committed by Luther. But he must learn to accept God's judgement. He took away his son and did not give my mother any other children except for myself. It is *His* will." She looked at Frances who parroted the words back to her.

"It is His will."

They continued walking, the other ladies behind them chattering about what they had heard the Princess say. They were loyal and strict Catholics, however, and would not repeat what they had heard.

"I am sorry. I just..."

"You are young." Mary spared a smile for her. "I know you and your family have been caught in the middle of this too."

Frances did not remind her that she was merely a year

older for in truth the Princess seemed wiser beyond her years. Despite her small stature, she had a domineering presence that inspired silence in those in her company.

While she was witty and funny in conversation, she still carried herself with the gravitas of knowing that she was her father's heir and that one day she would inherit the crown of England.

~

Their happy retreat to Windsor did not last long. The King and Anne wished to return to the Palace, but apparently Anne did not wish to find the Queen and Princess still living there.

Frances watched her mother rage. "How could he send you away? Why is he listening to that vile woman? If I could I would speak to him"

"Mary, sit down." Catherine looked heartbroken but did not voice her anger like her sister-in-law was doing.

"No!" She continued marching about the room.

"I fear that I shall be separated from my daughter, Mary, now permanently," the Queen went on. "She is to go to Richmond while I am to go to the More."

"You must..."

"What must I do?" Now Catherine's tone was harsh. "What can I possibly do? I must obey my husband and King."

"I shall take letters from you to her. I promise you shall not be separated for long. My brother would not be so cruel."

"No, perhaps he wouldn't but she would." Catherine

paused. "And she has promised him the world. What would he not do for her?"

"But she cannot have assurances. He cannot be such a fool to believe that she can deliver him the moon."

"Mary!" Catherine reproved her for her words.

Mary put a hand over her mouth, not believing she had uttered those words herself. She collapsed into an armchair and Frances ran over.

"Are you alright, Mother?" She saw Mary was pale. "Do you need anything?"

"I need to lie down in my rooms. Help me up, Frances." She held out her arm to her.

Frances turned to her aunt for permission to leave. She was walking over to them, concern painted across her face.

"Shall I send for a physician, Mary?"

"N-o, I should be fine. Too much is happening. Though I have no right to complain." Leaning on Frances, she stood.

Frances could feel how wobbly her mother's legs were beneath her.

"Frances, once you see your mother to her rooms, please summon Princess Mary to see me immediately. She cannot leave before she has seen me. No matter what they have ordered."

Frances nodded.

～

With Queen and Princess gone, Windsor felt abandoned and devoid of life. Frances and her mother had their personal servants and her mother's companions, but they all ate quietly in their room rather than the empty great hall.

Soon after the Queen's departure, the King's servants began to trickle in. They helped the permanent servants begin preparing the palace for his arrival. Sheets were changed, mantelpieces dusted. Then the King was finally there and Windsor witnessed a slew of activity as the noble men and women accompanying him piled in, trying to find rooms for themselves.

The chamberlain was kept busy making sure everyone was assigned to correct quarters according to rank.

What shocked Frances was that the Queen's own rooms had been reopened and given to the Boleyn woman for her use.

Seeing as her mother was still bedridden, a pain in her chest kept her from exerting herself too much, they avoided her.

Her father came to visit as soon as he heard of his wife's condition, and the King sent his own physician to see her.

"Shall I open Suffolk Place for you, my love?" he asked, looking at her pale complexion with obvious concern on his face.

"I shall recover." Her voice was weak, however.

"Mother, the court will only get busier. It would be easier for you to rest in your own house and not be stressed either." Frances tried to persuade her, seeing her father's exasperation.

"Fine, seeing as you two have colluded against me."

They were moved slowly first by barge and then by litter to Suffolk Place where her mother could rest. Frances was her constant companion, though they seemed to grate on each other's nerves at each step. Finally, her mother summoned Katherine Willoughby to join them.

"At least with her here, you will leave me alone, and she will be able to play some music for me."

"Mother, I am always happy to play for you," Frances said.

"You don't play half as well." Mary did not hold back her sharp tongue. "And I am not well enough to bear listening to your attempts."

Frances ignored her mother. It was true that Katherine offered some reprieve from her mother's temper. Katherine could mollify Mary, and, in the mornings, they were able to go for a ride.

~

Her father made an appearance a week later to check on them. Mary was now well enough to sit in her solar and sew, though she preferred to play the lute or listen to musicians. She was also intent on redecorating her rooms, claiming she was bored of looking at the same hangings after so many days spent confined to her bed.

"Do you have anything in blue?" she inquired and the man provided a few samples for her to choose from.

After studying them, she approved of a blue satin cloth inlaid with silver embroidery of the fleur-de-lys.

"Shall we become French now?" Frances heard her father joke from the entrance.

"Ha ha." Her mother didn't even spare him a glance. "I am the Dowager Queen of France, you know."

"When you are free later, I would like to speak to you," he continued.

"I shall send Frances to let you know."

"Very well. Please, remember we have two daughters' dowries to pay for before you decide to redo the whole house." He winked at Frances, whose heart skipped a beat.

Was this what he wanted to talk to her mother about? Had he come to discuss plans for her wedding? She prayed that Eleanor hadn't made a better match.

The rest of the day she felt as though there was something lodged in her throat. She cursed her mother's vanity and lack of interest. She had not gone to see her father until well into the afternoon, and they were still locked up in his study together.

Katherine was not much help either. Every little noise she made seemed to irk Frances, and she snapped at her more than a few times.

When they all sat down for a private family meal with the senior members of the household dining with them as well, Frances felt she would burst soon.

"You are barely touching your food," Mary scolded her. "Eat something or excuse yourself. You look so pale you better not be coming down with something."

"I-I... Mother, am I to be married?" The question leapt off her tongue before she could stop it.

Her father choked on a bite of venison.

"The impertinence!" Mary declared loudly.

It was her father who stopped her going into a full tirade.

"Dearest, I suppose it would not harm her to know."

"Not here though, surely." Mary was all sweetness for him. Her thick lashes batting at him innocently.

"Yes, I suppose it can wait." Charles ran a hand through

his beard. "You can come to my study after dinner and we shall discuss this then."

Frances stopped herself from protesting and merely nodded. Under the table Katherine squeezed her hand reassuringly.

A warm fire greeted Frances as she entered the wood paneled study. Her mother was sitting in a great winged chair as though it was a throne from which she would pass judgement. Her father was sifting through some letters at his desk.

She dropped into a low curtsey, hoping to have performed it gracefully enough.

"So, Frances, you might as well know that later this summer you shall move to the Marchioness of Dorset's house. You are to enter her household to complete your education and training as a great lady of the realm," her father said kindly as ever.

But this wasn't what Frances was expecting to hear. What of her marriage?

"I would be pleased to obey you, but why am I to go, my lord father?"

It was her mother who answered. "Obviously, silly cow, you have been betrothed to her son Henry Grey and you shall be married once you are older. She has requested you to stay with her."

"Mary, you don't have to be rude." Charles admonished her with a look.

"It is a good match for you. Henry is the Marquess of Dorset and he comes from a good family. His mother accompanied your mother to France for her first wedding. She shall be kind and treat you well," he reassured her.

But this wasn't what Frances was concerned about. She never received the gentlest treatment from her own mother. Only Queen Catherine ever treated her kindly.

"Where shall I live?"

"Bradgate House."

"And Eleanor? Has she been betrothed?"

"No, not officially. We are considering Henry Clifford..."

"...the Earl of Cumberland?" Frances finished and then blushed for she had interrupted her father.

"Yes."

"I see." Internally, Frances was celebrating that she was marrying higher than Eleanor, though not by much.

Mary seemed to grasp this and smiled slyly between her daughter and husband.

"Seems she's more ambitious than I thought."

Frances wasn't sure this was a compliment.

"How come I did not know? I thought, perhaps, you were considering a French prince for me."

Her mother's laugh filled the room.

"Do you think we'd consider you in every decision? You are our daughter and you shall wed where we bid you. I was married for the sake of my family and I did not have a say. Just be grateful your husband is of the same age as you."

"I am sorry." Frances could find her frown though.

"It is a good match," her father repeated, even though he didn't have to. "He is in favor with the King, and I am sure he will bring you to court often."

"He should be, considering it is your father who shall be paying his household expenses until he reaches his majority," Mary added, the contempt oozing out with each word.

"You are dismissed, Frances," her father said, trying to avoid an argument.

Frances bowed and said good night.

She thought she would be skipping back to her rooms after finding out who she was married to, but instead she was filled with more apprehension than anything. She had hoped she would make a more illustrious marriage. Perhaps to a Duke at least.

She wracked her brain thinking what she knew about Henry Grey. She must have seen him at court once or twice, though she never interacted with him before. He was a distant relation of hers. They shared a great-grandmother in Elizabeth Woodville. However, his grandfather had not been the son of a King but rather the first son of her first marriage to Sir John Grey of Groby. He didn't really have any royal blood in his veins. That in itself was disappointing.

She did not think he was particularly sportive or brave either. She couldn't remember seeing him on the lists, so perhaps he never took part in jousting. But he was likely among those young men who hung around her uncle the King.

She wondered if he too wrote poems about Anne Boleyn.

"Frances?" Katherine was waving a hand in front of her face.

Frances shook her head coming out of her thoughts. "Huh?"

"I asked you if you were alright?" Katherine looked concerned.

"I am... I was just thinking."

"Did it go well?" Katherine pressed.

"I am to go live with the Marquess of Dorset as I am betrothed to her son."

"Which one?"

"Henry, who inherited after his father passed away."

"Have you ever seen him?"

"No, but I suppose I shall see him if I am to live at Bradgate."

"I wonder if he is handsome," Katherine mused. "He must not be old."

Frances was wondering about other things. Was he wealthy? Would she be able to have nice dresses and jewels?

～

Margaret Grey had been born Margaret Wotton to a Knight from Kent. She had done very well marrying the Marquess of Dorset. After all, she had barely had much a dowry, though her brothers were well connected in Parliament. Frances thought rudely that she must have been an ambitious woman to manage to squeeze herself into such a position of power.

More than that, she seemed keen to be friendly with everyone. It did not take long for Frances to realize Margaret was on friendly terms with the Boleyns.

Only a person of low class would agree to associate with them. She had thought that her mother was sending her to live with a dear friend for she had accompanied her to France, but it was clear there was no tender feelings between the two of them. In fact, it seemed to amuse

Margaret that she now had command of the daughter of Mary Tudor, to whom she had bowed and scraped to.

Frances could not disobey her future mother-in-law. She thought of Katherine and knew now how she must have felt when she first arrived at Suffolk Place. But she had been kind to Katherine.

In the Grey household she was treated coldly.

Two of the younger sons were still in the schoolroom and young Mary Grey was in the nursery barely able to walk, but she felt pushed aside for them.

Her rooms were comfortable but nowhere near as grand as those she had at Suffolk Place or Westhorpe. She thought longingly of her fine Turkish carpets and the clothes she would borrow from her mother on special occasions. Margaret Grey did not seem inclined to provide her with the same treatment.

Every day seemed to go the same. They would attend Mass, hear a preacher give a talk, depending on the weather go take a stroll around the gardens and then have an afternoon meal before retiring to do chores from sewing shirts to working on embroidery to other menial tasks.

Margaret, like Frances's mother before her, seemed to enjoy insulting Frances at every turn.

She was sure Margaret felt she was taking her under her wing, but Frances knew how a household should be run. She did not need to listen to Margaret. The first thing she would do once she was married was to hire more servants. There was no need for them to spend the afternoon weaving wool. Couldn't they have some woman from the village do that? And didn't even Anne Boleyn hire a woman to sew shirts for the King?

Frances wouldn't demean herself with such lowly tasks.

"If you applied yourself better you could become good enough with a needle that you could gift this to the King himself." Margaret was frowning as she examined her latest attempt at black work on a collar. "The first few stitches are fine but I can tell you lost interest halfway through."

Frances had the decency to look abashed. "I shall redo it."

Margaret seemed to regard her for a few moments. "These sorts of skills are important for any young lady to possess. Your husband shall appreciate you for them more than for your ability to ride horses or play cards well."

Frances nodded, but she had to hide her face so Margaret wouldn't see the contempt there.

"Not all households live as large and freely as others." Frances knew she was having a go at her parents, who were notoriously extravagant.

"My son has placed us in debt when he refused to marry the Earl of Arundel's daughter. We have to pay the price now. You shall have to pay the price as well."

Frances gaped. "He was betrothed before?"

"Of course he was. If his father was still alive he would have made them marry. She was such a good girl. Very pretty and handy to have around."

Frances puffed out her chest, ready to retort that whoever this girl was she did not have the lineage she possessed.

"He was tempted though," Margaret went on, giving her a look of extreme displeasure.

"Not by me. I never met him before," Frances said indignantly.

"No, not by you — by power, by greed, by ambition." She shook her head. "You will find you are not enough to keep him happy."

"I do not know what you are insinuating, madam, but I will be a good wife to your son. He is lucky to have gained my hand in marriage," Frances said coolly.

Margaret looked ready to strike, but then sat back in her chair and regarded her as though seeing her for the first time.

"I have to congratulate your confidence. You are very sure of yourself. Perhaps you shall be well matched, seeing as both of you have airs of grandeur. It will lead you into trouble."

And that was the last Margaret said on the matter, though her comments continued to grate on Frances's mind long after the conversation.

Of course, her lineage would always be a major attraction. Frances was not a fool, but the fact that her mother-in-law had basically doomed them to a life of unhappiness terrified her. She knew enough about curses and prophecies to be nervous about her words. Would simply ill wishing them be enough to make her words come true? And what kind of mother was so mean to her own child and heir?

Though her mother constantly berated her, Frances knew that she would never say half the things Margaret said about her son on a daily basis. She was surprised she hadn't become terrified of her betrothed. The man Margaret described led her to imagine a short miserly man counting coins, but she had seen his portrait and knew that she was lying.

It was on days that Margaret was too busy for her

company that she found solace in the forest surrounding Bradgate. The trees were thick and green — the air fresh and the sky blue as she rode through the undergrowth on well-trodden paths.

The Marchioness of Dorset kept a large herd of deer on her park and rarely hunted them. Frances thought it was Margaret who was the miser.

On rainy days, she stayed inside writing letters to her mother and father as well as to Katherine who she sorely missed now that she was gone from her side. She wished to have a friend again. Perhaps once she was married then she could ask Katherine to come stay with her as a lady-in-waiting.

She daydreamed of showing Katherine the park and taking her around the pleasant palace gardens.

She did not complain of her treatment for she felt that was exactly what her mother-in-law wanted of her. She could picture what would happen in her mind. Either her mother would take her side and demand the Marchioness treat her better, which might lead to the Marchioness deciding to convince her son to put her aside, or her mother would be angry at her for complaining.

There would be no winning either way.

If the betrothal was set aside, who would want her after that? She might be seen as spoiled goods, and she wouldn't put it past Margaret to spread vile rumors about her. Was it her fault she was used to certain luxuries? She felt sure that Margaret was depriving her of them on purpose.

She just wanted to punish her son by punishing his betrothed. It was no wonder he never visited.

She had hoped she would catch sight of him, so she

could tell Margaret that she had lied about her son. But there was no news from him. He had never even written her a note or sent her a message. She had seen the signed contract of their betrothal. He had signed his name above hers so she knew he knew of her existence.

Was he not curious about his future bride?

She thought of his spiteful mother again. No doubt, if she had remained with her parents, he would have paid her a visit there, but, here at Bradgate, he must feel unwelcome and stayed away.

This was Margaret's doing again. She was being held captive and she had not even realized it. Perhaps she had been the one to stall their wedding. Her mother had been married at her age after all, so she wasn't too young.

She took these thoughts to bed with her every night. At Mass she would pray to be rescued or for some reprieve.

She was tired of being drilled on numbers and the accounts of the household. How much wheat was produced, how much wool, why should she care? Wasn't this the reason why they hired a steward to manage their affairs?

At length, her prayers were answered. A messenger bearing the royal coat of arms entered the presence chamber and presented a summons to the Marchioness.

She broke the seal gingerly, as if she did not wish to and scanned the message with her beady eyes. Frances leaned towards her to see what it said but the older woman rolled up the scroll.

"Thank you, we shall be attending. It would be an honor." She motioned for her lord chamberlain to tip the man.

Frances could not wait, and, the minute he left, she asked what was happening.

"We are going to Windsor. We have been invited to witness the investiture of the Lady Anne Boleyn." She declared this without the familiar resentment usually present when one talked of Anne in her presence.

"And what title is she going to get?" Frances scowled.

"Marchioness of Pembroke."

Frances froze mid-step. A Marchioness? That woman would be made a Marchioness? Was there no end to cruelty in this world? Was the King still hoping to marry her after all this time? Was he not content with dismissing his wife and daughter from court?

Margaret had paused at the end of the hallway, obviously noting she had stopped moving. She smiled knowingly at her.

"You shall be attending as well, and I seem to need to remind you to smile. If you don't and you bring any sort of trouble on my head, I'll have you sent back to your parents and annul your betrothal faster than you can blink. Is that understood?"

Frances was shaken and could only nod.

"Good."

～

Her mother was thankfully absent at the investiture. Another key person who was absent was the Duke of Norfolk's own wife, who had refused point blank to carry Anne's train.

Frances smiled to herself, remembering the kind letters

she passed along to Queen Catherine. After all this time, she had not abandoned her friend.

Frances watched Anne's procession to the King with a grim hope the woman would trip on her way. She was followed by her uncle, the French ambassador and several heralds. Garter carried her Letters Patent of creation on a pillow as though they were fragments of the Holy Cross.

Frances felt dowdy beside Anne in her crimson red sur-coat. She looked at the ermine with particular distaste. Only a select few were allowed to wear it, herself included. She hated to think she would be allowed to now.

Besides her fantastic dress, she was also decked out in new jewels as well as some very recognizable ones.

"Is that Queen Catherine's..." she whispered, but her future mother-in-law pinched her so she stopped.

"Do not mention Queen Catherine."

"But she is wearing the Queen's jewels!" Couldn't she see how ridiculous this was?

Margaret looked at her as though to say: *and what is wrong with that?*

Frances looked back towards Anne with a barely concealed contempt as they walked behind her. Finally, they reached the great presence chamber, and she spotted her father standing prominently beside the King.

Anne moved forward and knelt before the King. Frances could only imagine her grim satisfaction. Garter handed the Letters Patent to Bishop Gardiner who read them out loud.

Frances was seeing red by this point. Why was Anne receiving a title in her own right? Did she, as one of the few Tudor descendants, not deserve one herself? She thought of her aunt, deprived of her jewels and her cousin kept away from court without even a single marriage prospect.

She managed to collect herself as the whole court processed into the Chapel Royal to celebrate a special Mass. The occasion was further marked by a signed peace treaty with France.

Frances could not even begin to comprehend. In her mind, she was already penning the letter to her mother telling her of everything she had seen.

A day after, they headed back to Bradgate and Frances was not sorry to leave the court and its madness behind.

She was not envious that many of them would travel to France with the King, for Anne Boleyn would also be there and she refused to curtsey to her. She was now technically of higher rank than Frances and she was sure the King would only increase her status.

It made her even madder that during their short visit to court, she had been so distracted by Anne she had not even thought to look for her betrothed.

$\sim$

Time passed slowly for Frances.

Margaret did not keep her abreast of the news from court. She had to rely on maids' gossip, which was hardly reliable. There were rumors that the King had indeed married Anne, for they were taking their time returning to London. But Frances could not believe any of this. She knew she should be following in her mother-in-law's shoes and be loyal to the Boleyn faction but she could not bring herself to do it.

She thought of how her father would be happy if their family could fully reconcile to the King and be friendly with the Boleyns who had shown how deadly their displeasure could be. Perhaps, above all, he had hoped this marriage would make her change her mind.

But then she thought of her mother who had barely managed to speak to Anne without distaste. Her mother who was made ill by her friend's banishment.

She couldn't bear to like that woman or pay her any respect. Somehow no one asked for her opinion. She was merely required to obey.

She wondered if her betrothed thought as she did. She imagined he did.

By November they had confirmation that the King and Anne had taken up residence at Greenwich.

"Are we to join the court for Christmas?" Frances inquired one cloudy afternoon. She had not been able to escape her mother-in-law's rooms to go hawking.

"No, I do not believe we will. We shall pass a quiet Christmas here, and I have received news from your parents."

This truly surprised Frances. Seeing her eagerness Margaret seemed happy enough to postpone the news for as long as possible.

"We have decided that it would be appropriate for you to wed in March and your sister is to be officially betrothed."

"I am? She is?" Frances gasped. This was her chance for freedom.

"So, naturally, I would like to have a few extra months with you alone so you may learn as much as you can. I am

113

afraid I have not had enough time, but the King has given your father his blessing on the match and my son seems eager enough."

"And my wedding? Shall the King attend?"

Margaret looked like she wanted to laugh at her audacity, but then she seemed to remember who she was.

"I don't think the King will be able to attend, but fear not, your mother has written to me and informed me that you would be married from Suffolk Place, so perhaps you shall have your opportunity for glory."

"I shall have to go prepare a few weeks before then. After all, I need to be adequately prepared," Frances pressed.

"Not a moment sooner than when I think you are ready," Margaret stipulated.

Frances did not complain. "I shall write to my mother."

She rushed from the rooms to her little writing desk before Margaret could forbid her.

Immediately, she began asking her mother about what the wedding preparations would be like. Would she have an Archbishop say the ceremony? Was there perhaps a Cardinal who would marry them? She didn't think there were any Cardinals left in England but why not try? She also asked about dresses and how many she would be allowed to get.

By the time she was done, the sun had set. Her letter was filled with mostly questions and demands, so she thought it prudent to ask after her mother's health and to give Eleanor her congratulations on her upcoming betrothal.

Then she wrote a letter to Katherine telling her she

would have to be her Lady and carry her train on her wedding day. She told her not to be jealous of her good fortune.

Since the roads were still good and had not been covered by snow, the replies piled in quickly enough.

Her mother's letter was dictated to Eleanor, who had written down every word their mother had said. Frances blushed red to know that Eleanor heard their mother scolding her for vanity and reminding her to be obedient. The rest of the letter was much more promising.

Her father had agreed to supply her with a wardrobe of ten gowns, with accompanying accessories, in addition to a splendid wedding dress.

Her mother wrote she had already selected the fabrics that would best suit her. For her wedding dress, she had settled on a beautiful patterned white and gold silk imported from Italy at great cost, she added. Frances could picture her mother's pointed look, expecting gratitude for this generosity, which Frances would be more than happy to give. The gown would be measured to her general size and adjusted once she arrived.

Beyond this, her mother went on about the great responsibility that would be hers now and that she would have to obey her husband in everything.

Above all, she was not to shame their family.

Frances could only imagine how dazzling she would seem to Henry Grey when he finally saw her.

She was suddenly glad they had not met, though she had found his portrait in the gallery upstairs and often paused to examine it. She thought she saw a smile beneath the serious exterior. A secret smile just for her.

True to Margaret's word, Christmas was a miserable affair. They burned a Yule Log in the great hall and enjoyed a small feast with the servants. The elder Grey sisters and their husbands paid them a visit too. For this Margaret decided to cull a few beasts from the herd of deer that she so coveted.

They feasted on venison and pies as hired musicians played. There was no dancing or masking, however, and Frances could only rely on Katherine's letters for any gossip of substance.

It seemed the King had ordered renovations to be made on the Tower, and then specifically the Queen's quarters. Everyone believed Queen Catherine would be sent to the Tower, but, in fact, it was Anne who stayed there a few nights.

During this time, the King also awarded her gold plate for her household. It was rumored by now that they had married in secret. Katherine feared for the Queen.

Frances could not bring herself to consider the luxuries heaped on Anne, although after her creation as the Marchioness of Pembroke she should have hardly been surprised.

Then, in a letter at the end of January, Katherine told her the most scandalous thing of all.

Anne was rumored to be pregnant.

Cranmer had been named Archbishop and there was much haste being made in Parliament to hurry along the matter of the King's divorce. Katherine stressed that these were rumors and she did not believe them herself.

Frances could not wait to leave Bradgate and head back to Suffolk Place. She would see what she could discover for herself.

～

Indeed, the whole of England was scandalized.

Frances traveled by litter to Suffolk Place in small stages. Margaret had accompanied her so she was not spared her commentary. At each stop they made, there seemed to be fresh news. Many were eager to share what they heard.

"The King had obtained permission from Rome to marry Anne."

"That Lady was with child and it was created in sin."

"The King was a bigamous with two wives."

"The Lady was to be crowned Queen."

Frances did not get a clear narrative until at last they arrived at her home. If her future mother-in-law was impressed with its grandeur, she did a good job hiding it. But once inside the familiar doors, Frances could escape her overbearing presence.

She rushed to hug her mother, who she was surprised to find was still confined to her rooms.

"Oh, I am fine most days but this foul weather has made me weak. The doctors say it is better I stay in bed."

Seeing as there was no reason to worry, she asked her mother what was going on at court. Her mother, though confined, seemed to possess a powerful spy network or at the very least was well informed by her husband.

"It's almost certain he has married her. Though I doubt

it was with the Pope's permission. She was heard declaring she would go on pilgrimage to Our Lady of Walsingham." Mary gave her daughter a knowing look.

"She is with child?" Frances was scandalized.

"Probably."

"Surely, the child's birth would always be in question. It's too soon. Is the marriage even legal?"

"You must never say that aloud," Mary scolded her. "But if it is a boy it shall be legitimate for sure and we shall all have to bow and scrape to that Boleyn woman."

~

Preparations for the wedding were underway. The best gold and silver plate was brought out of the treasury for the occasion. Her father wanted to show his opulence and her mother was never one to hide from the spotlight.

Her dress was as splendid as her mother described. It was flattering on her too, giving her skin a healthy pinkish glow. They spent days carefully sewing pearls into it. She would be dressed as finely as the Princess Mary.

Katherine had remained silent about accompanying her once she was married.

"I don't think I can go. I should stay here. I don't think they'd let me go anyways. I am your father's ward."

Frances had frowned but no amount of pouting made her get her way.

At length, she dropped the matter entirely and the two of them discussed happier matters from the clothes she received to the horse her father promised her she could pick from the stables. He also promised to give her a pair of fine greyhounds since she had seemed to take to hunting so much.

With so much wedding planning underway, there was hardly any time for her to dwell on her groom. She thought of him with a feeling of happy anticipation. When they moved back to Bradgate, he would surely rescue her from the clutches of his mother.

It turned out that the King and most of the nobles of the realm were attending her wedding, which was being postponed until April now.

She was smiling gleefully as she informed her soon-to-be mother-in-law. But if Margaret was impressed she hid it very well. In fact, she disapproved of the extravagant cost of the wedding.

"This could pay for food over the winter," she said, when she saw the pearls on her dress.

"This is merely a dress befitting her station," her mother interjected.

There was nothing Margaret could say, seeing as Mary outranked her by far.

Frances was enjoying her mother's protection for once, but she wasn't sure how long this could last. After all, what would happen when she left for her marital home? It did not seem like there were any plans being made for her to go to court, not that she would want to serve Anne Boleyn, and her mother had made no mention of her staying with her either.

It didn't take her long to notice that her mother often retreated back to her rooms or stayed in bed for much of the days.

"Are you not well, Mother?" she asked tentatively one

morning as they watched the carts full of meat and fish being brought in. With the wedding only a few days away their larders were being filled and the cooks kept busy in the kitchens day and night.

"It was a hard journey for me to come to London from Westhorpe. The doctors say I have an ague. It comes and goes but leaves me feeling weak."

Her mother's condition shocked her, but she quickly convinced herself that the best doctors in the Kingdom were treating her and that soon she would be well, especially when she returned to the fresh air of the country.

At last, the day arrived for her wedding. Already Suffolk Place was packed to the brim with visiting nobles and their families. The King would arrive on that morning to see her walking to the altar in the Suffolk chapel.

Where she had been anxious being the center of attention a few years ago, now she reveled in the attention she was getting. The gifts she received went a long way to stifling her nerves as well. She almost forgot that after today she would cease to be Lady Frances Brandon and become the Marchioness Frances Grey.

Her mother was in high spirits that morning, and her sister and Katherine were there to help her get ready.

A warm bath was drawn and she was washed in scented oils. Her hair was perfumed with rose water. Then piece by piece she was dressed in the elaborate gown and its undergarments. The new smock was the softest she had ever owned. The cuffs and neckline were embroidered in black thread. The crest of her family was etched into top of the cuffs visible over the sleeves of her gown.

Her mother had done it herself, and she expressed sincere gratitude.

Her headdress was one her mother had worn during her short time as Queen of France. Made with black and white satin, it was surprisingly lightweight despite its impressive display of jewels. The tear-shaped pearls encircled the hood encapsulated in a gold setting, at the center a small gold rose to symbolize her Tudor heritage was sewn in by a goldsmith.

She twirled in her gown before her mother's looking mirror until she was ordered to stand still.

Before Frances knew it, there was no more time to study the jewels on her fingers or the sheen of her new gown. They rushed to the chapel where a large congregation awaited. She spotted the towering shape of her uncle, looking as Kingly as ever. He had a kind happy smile on his face when he saw her.

Then her eyes became fixed on her groom waiting in front of the priest. He seemed anxious as he fidgeted with the gold buttons of his coat. He was dressed in a matching costume of white and black satin.

He was not short and miserly. In fact, he seemed well proportioned and gave the appearance of a gentle man. Frances blushed to see he was looking at her too. His eyes raked her from her headdress down to her toes. She knew he was admiring her rich gown.

Her father led her down the aisle and handed her to the groom. She took his offered hand, and then, unable to bear it any longer, turned her attention to the priest who dressed in his formal garb.

The ceremony seemed to drone on and on. The heavy

smell of burning incense was threatening to make her sneeze. In an effort to distract herself, Frances took to thinking of the jousting and banquet afterwards. She couldn't wait to see what other presents they had received too.

And just like that it was over.

Frances had promised to obey, and he had promised to endow her with his goods. She didn't pay much attention to what she parroted back to the priest. She was itching to sit down or dance.

Suffolk Place had been transformed. Wine was being served freely, and, out in the courtyard, commoners were celebrating. They stopped to applaud them as they stepped out of the chapel followed by the King and her father at his heels.

Frances waved back to them, more than happy to hear from them that she made a beautiful bride. She looked to her husband and found he too was looking at the crowd and waving.

They were seated below the King and ate countless dishes of meats, fish and pies. For dessert there were two enormous marchpane cakes. One had her coat of arms and the other her husband's.

She loved the sweet rich taste.

After all the food, she was in no mood for dancing, but her husband led her up for one dance at least, not taking no for an answer.

"We have to dance. The King is watching and it is expected of us. You wouldn't want to embarrass me before all these people, would you?" he whispered.

So obediently she stood, and joined the others. Trying

hard to smile but knowing she was grimacing as her stomach hurt from overeating. She was spared from dancing further as a troupe of maskers began to perform. Then an acrobat and a fool interrupted them, causing a minor brawl between the troupe leader and the fool, which left their noble guests laughing.

Frances was busy trying to soak it all in, when it struck her that perhaps she should speak to her husband. Watching him from the corner of her eyes, she suddenly felt shy. She didn't want to say the wrong thing, and he must have already gotten the wrong impression about her.

She wasn't a glutton.

It wasn't her fault that her mother had arranged for some of her favorite foods to be served to her. She hadn't eaten all morning either, as she had too many nerves to even think of swallowing down anything.

"Do you like Suffolk Place?" she finally asked. Then wondered if that was a strange question to ask. What did one say to one's husband? She thought of her mother and father who always spoke and never seemed to be awkward with one another.

"It's very grand," he replied unhelpfully.

"I've been staying at Bradgate, the park there is wonderful," she continued.

At this he seemed to perk up. "Do you like to hunt?"

"Yes, of course. My father has promised to give me a new horse and a pair of greyhounds. Perhaps we can go hunting together? Your mother has not let me hunt, so I have been restricted to merely riding."

"My mother is..." he paused searching for way to describe her. "...an unnatural mother. She still has control

123

over my lands until I come into my majority. I would call her greedy, but she is in fact just petty. She is fine spending my money on fine clothes for herself. Meanwhile, she has the gall to restrict my allowance."

"She told me," Frances leaned towards him conspiratorially. "She seems quite spiteful and did not treat me well. I am glad I shall have you at my side."

He seemed puzzled by this.

"I shall most likely be at court. Your father has yet to settle a place on us where we can live. In the meantime, you will just have to live at Bradgate."

"But your mother..."

"Unfortunately, I can do nothing until I am older," he was frowning again. "You should talk to your father. Perhaps he can give us a London house and you can stay there. I shall be at court most of the time." She saw him looking towards the King and her father who were cajoling with their arms around one another as they called out to the fool.

"Or perhaps the King, your uncle, will reward us with some gift. I wouldn't mind another title. Perhaps some more lands," he looked at her expectantly.

"I-I rarely, speak to him."

"You shall speak to him more. You are his niece. I am sure he will be generous," he took her hand and placed a kiss on the back of her hand, giving her a sweet smile. "We shall do very well the two of us."

Frances's throat was dry. She wasn't sure she could do what he asked. More than that, how would he react if she couldn't deliver?

Her mother and father always talked about how they

had little money to go around. Her mother had her dower payments from France, but those were unreliable and her father was in heavy debt to the crown, so he was struggling to maintain his estate. This wedding was an exuberant expense for them.

She was sure that Margaret had more money lying around than her own parents. Could they not appeal to his mother now that he was married to increase their allowance?

It was well passed dark when she was escorted by her mother, sister and mother-in-law to her wedding chamber. They watched the maids undress her and put her to bed to await her husband.

At length he arrived quite drunk and wobbling on his feet. His groom of the bedchamber had to help him into bed, pretending nothing was amiss.

With that, the priest came to say a blessing but her husband interrupted the serious moment by deciding to let out a loud belch, which set him and his friends laughing. Frances was mortified. Seeing him like this, she could see nothing but a rude child. This was far from the image of the Prince she had imagined.

She soon also realized how alone they suddenly were. They had barely spoken. When thinking of her wedding, she had barely focused on him or what would come after the feasting. She was scared to move and attract his attention as he was fighting with the blankets beside her. Her mother had been incredibly vague about what would happen when they were alone.

She knew from gossiping maids that a man and woman had to sleep together to have children. From what she had seen of animals in the countryside, she knew there must be more to this than just sleeping beside one another.

It still left her feeling queasy and she hoped that he would not attempt anything tonight. But it seemed that her husband had other plans. His hand had crept its way over to hers.

"You seem lost in thought," he mumbled. "Your hair smells nice."

She saw he had rolled over so now his face was on her spread-out hair.

She supposed this was his attempt at being seductive as he inched his way towards her. She tried her best not to pull away or look repulsed, but he did smell strongly of spirits. She thought of how meticulously her mother had prepared her this morning and felt that he was ruining everything.

"Thank you, I suppose."

His smile was crooked as he leaned forward and placed a kiss on her brow.

She waited for something else to happen but nothing did. He had laid back down and fallen into a deep slumber.

She was dreading the morning.

She was too embarrassed to think of her maids coming in and pulling her out of bed to find her with her husband. She was mortified thinking of what her mother would say.

She was a Marchioness now, but she felt more like an animal in the field. With these thoughts whirling through her head she could not sleep.

Beside her, Henry was sleeping so soundly he had begun snoring heavily. He was clearly pleased with himself. She wished he would have had the decency to get up and leave if he wanted to sleep.

She had done her duty and welcomed him to her bed. Did she have to put up with him afterwards too?

Sometime after, when she felt she could not stand it anymore, she got up and wiped herself clean with a cloth and water from a washing basin nearby. The dancing and celebrations had left her sweaty. She relished the feeling of the cool water on her skin.

It then struck her that now that she was married she might become pregnant.

The thought was not particularly pleasant for her. She was too young to start having children. She didn't want to get plump and fat, she wanted to dance and go hunting.

She looked over to her husband again. He had said they could go hunting together.

She returned to bed but slept on top of the sheets and waited for morning.

~

Frances was standing beside her husband as they played bowls in the palace gardens at Greenwich.

"The King has said he will make you a Knight of the Bath. He told my father this morning." She looked up at him, expecting him to smile.

"Nothing about a title?"

"No." She hesitated. "But it's a great honor. I am sure you shall receive other shows of favor too. You have become a great favorite at court. Everyone says so."

He scoffed and threw his bowl, hitting her own out of the way as he managed to nearly touch her cone.

She let him win the next round too.

"I am sorry..." She waited for him to say something.

He finally turned to her, pasting what she recognized as a forced smile on his face. "Of course, it is just I am tired of being at the mercy of others. My mother holds my lands, we have to turn to your father for charity and your uncle does not take me seriously."

"My father is happy to support us." Frances touched his arm. "We shall prevail upon your mother to increase your allowance. Soon you shall enter your majority and then you can kick her off your lands."

This seemed to soothe him a bit but just as quickly he was frowning again.

"But I don't want this to continue for another five years."

She was at a cross roads as she watched him kicking his feet around. She could continue trying to reassure him or she could let her temper fly at him.

She chose the latter.

"It is not my fault you cannot stand up to your mother! My father has been more than generous. He is allowing us to use Suffolk Place." She did not remind him of the countless other gifts her father had given them, including a purse of one hundred pounds.

Now she looked at him reprovingly. "I don't have everything I want either. Do you think I do not see the gifts lavished on my sister Eleanor by her betrothed? Am I not entitled to jewels, and new gowns? My mother is the Dowager Queen of France, whereas yours is the lowly daughter of a Knight."

He took a step back shocked at her outspokenness.

"How dare you!" Now he moved forward, but she did not balk in the face of his anger. She met his anger face on.

They were preparing to square off again when they were interrupted by the sound of footsteps. Realizing how inappropriate being caught in the middle of a row would be, they stepped away from each other, and Frances tried to soothe her angry expression into one of indifference.

It was Mary Boleyn who came strolling through with a stranger Frances couldn't quite place.

They quickly excused themselves. Frances was trying her best to be polite as she had no wish to antagonize the sister of the soon-to-be Queen of England.

The Parliament had voted. Cranmer had debated. And they all declared that the King was never truly married to Queen Catherine. The Princess Mary was now no longer a Princess, but the King's illegitimate daughter. No better than Henry Fitzroy, the King's bastard son.

Frances wasn't sure how such a thing was possible. She kept her head down and followed her parents lead.

Her mother had returned to Westhorpe to recover, and she did not want to trouble her.

It was her own father that took the news to her aunt. The whole court knew that she had refused to be addressed as the Princess Dowager. She exclaimed that she was still the Queen. Her father had yelled at her and she had fled into her rooms.

The rumors continued to claim that her father had tried to force the former Queen to come out of her rooms, but she did not believe her father capable of such cruelty. He was not hot tempered, and he had been loyal to her.

Once they were inside the castle, Frances made her way

to her own room while Henry claimed to have to see someone about something. She watched him go, knowing that they would make up sooner or later. They were both quick to anger, and she had not learned to defer to him as the church claimed a good wife should.

Her confessor actually scolded her when she had asked for advice. It was her duty to please her husband and take care of him — not to argue with him. This had made her want to argue with the priest, but she was wise enough to hold her tongue.

~

Her father had arranged for new rooms for them at Suffolk Place. She had retreated here to avoid the preparations being made for Anne's coronation. Her mother had been right, the woman was indeed pregnant and Frances wrote to tell her so.

Frances was sure that if Anne hadn't loosened her gowns and been sporting an obvious bump, her constant gestures would give anyone a clear indication she was pregnant. One hand always seemed to go to her stomach as though she was carrying a heavy precious burden.

It made the King dote on her though she was more irritable than ever. Nothing seemed to please her, and she still railed against Queen Catherine though she was far away in Bedfordshire and could not harm her.

Frances could not understand what the King saw in her. She was decked in jewels and fine clothes, but that did not disguise the fact that she was now in her thirties. She was not the young attractive woman that had come to court from France.

Frances saw her as pale and sickly, but, while she was with child, who was to be the longed-for son and heir, she was the very best in the King's eyes.

Henry visited her on the rare occasion when he ran out of pocket money or felt the need to do his husbandly duty by her. With everyone talking about heirs, it seemed he wished for a child as well.

For her part, Frances did not mind she was taking her time getting with child. Since her husband stayed away and she was out of his mother's clutches, she had a freedom she had not enjoyed before.

She did not need to ask anyone permission to ride out. She could spend her money on what she wanted to. Though there was little of that for her to worry about. Her mother-in-law kept hold of the family fortune tightly.

She hoped that her and Henry would find a way to live amicably. Sometimes they were so good together, but other times they just got on each other's nerves.

Frances found herself reflecting on this a lot.

She wanted him to adore her the way the King seemed to adore Anne. She felt certain she was worthier of love. Perhaps they had gotten off on a rocky footing. She was too combative and he was too demanding.

She could not get him a title or the money he craved. She wouldn't even know how to ask. Her father was already annoyed that he had to supplement their income but felt it was an investment in the long run. She also did not feel it should be her responsibility to get him the positions he craved.

She felt strongly she had been meant for a better match. But she could appreciate that he was young and not unsightly. He had good connections and the King approved of him.

Perhaps he had not wanted her to make a brilliant match.

She still remembered how the Duke of Buckingham had been executed for raising up an army against the King. He had a strong claim to the throne and the King had thought it would be safer to chop off his head.

She decided she would speak to her father the next time she saw him to make sure her husband would get a place during Anne's coronation. It would not mean anything to her, but she knew it might go a long way to placate him.

~

Katherine's letter came as a shock to her. Her mother was bedridden and sicker than ever. She reassured Frances that the doctors were treating her well and trying to find a cure. There was a chance she could rally.

"Henry, what does she mean by there is a chance she could improve?" Frances pleaded. "You don't think she is…"

"I'm sure it is just her overreaction. You cannot read into every word or turn of phrase. She will mend."

"Perhaps I should go to her." Frances propped herself up on her elbows on the bed.

"It would be a long journey and you would miss the coronation. You know my mother is coming and demands you attend too. I demand it as well."

He must have seen she was preparing to argue and he tempered his words.

"It's important for you to attend. It would be noticed if you weren't here. It's hardly a secret that your mother still supports the Dowager Princess."

"Queen," Frances whispered under her breath, but he did not hear her.

"Say you will stay," he pleaded. "You can go visit your mother after the coronation. Besides it'll be another chance for you to wear your gown."

Frances had managed to calm down by now and thought the opportunity to attend her first coronation would be an exciting opportunity she could not miss, even if it was for Anne Boleyn.

She fell asleep that night dreaming of outshining Anne as they processed through the streets of London.

~

Her husband stood proud in his coat trimmed with ermine supplied by the royal wardrobe. Tomorrow he would walk as the King's sword bearer in the coronation procession from the Tower to Westminster. Frances would merely be one of the high-ranking ladies following behind Anne's litter. She had not wished to play an active role.

Anne wished to eclipse Catherine's coronation by making sure hers was even grander. Even Frances had been sent clothes from the royal wardrobe to borrow for the day.

Her father was named as Lord High Steward, and he was in charge of the nobles and assigning their duties during the coronation. Cranmer was planning the procession, and, in an effort to improve on the route, he added a route by water. The whole ceremony was going to take four days in total.

Frances would rather be resting at Bradgate. She watched from the banks of the river as the procession passed them by. She would not have any role to play until tomorrow.

The barge of the Lord Mayor of London led the water pageant. All the barges were splendidly decorated with banners and garlands. A great boat with the head of a dragon spewed fire every once in a while, as the people on the bank cheered.

Frances had seen such displays before and was not impressed.

Anne was dressed in cloth of gold and was enjoying herself in the newly decorated barge that had once belonged to Queen Catherine. The bishops and lords were in their own barge escorting hers.

Frances wondered how she could stand to use stolen goods. They must be cursed.

The next day she watched proudly from the sidelines as her husband was created a Knight of the Bath, just as she had promised him he would be. Her husband was dressed in a costume of violet trimmed with fur. He knelt before the King and was dubbed.

Soon after, she was ushered over to the other ladies of the realm who would be pulled by chariots. Behind Anne.

Anne was a blaze of white from her horses to the litter to her clothes. Against all this white was her long dark hair let down over her shoulders. The only adornment on her head was a simple gold circlet encrusted with jewels.

The judges who had made all this possible appeared and were taking their places in the procession. Anne thanked them from her litter.

"Thank you for all the honor you have done me this day."

Frances had to keep from laughing. She owed them her very crown; without the arguments of the lawyers there would be no wedding ceremony.

Anne would likely keep them all gainfully employed.

They stopped along the way to see the various pageants set up along the route.

At Gracechurch street Holbein had designed Mount Parnassus. A man dressed as Apollo greeted her and the Nine Muses beside him all had verses prepared. Frances couldn't help but note the theme of reform coursing through all the pageants. Were they truly turning away from Rome?

The poets promised nothing but a golden future and many sons for the new Queen. She managed well all things considering, but Frances had seen how relieved she was when they finally reached Westminster and she went to the Queen's chamber to change.

It was late in the evening now, and she looked for her husband but he was out of sight.

"There you are." Her mother-in-law had found her. "That was splendid, was it not?"

"Yes, who knew she had the stomach for such a public performance." Frances's jab did not go unnoticed.

"And where is my son?" Margaret asked, knowing full well he must have gone off already.

"He left to celebrate with his peers. He was made a Knight of the Bath today, as I am sure you have seen."

"Yes, such an honor. I am sure he is very pleased."

Frances nodded. Both women knew this wasn't quite true.

The following day Anne was finally crowned by Cranmer.

Frances had not accompanied her up to the altar but after the *Te Deum* was sung and Anne went to give the customary offering to St. Edward's shrine, she, along with all the other peeresses of the realm, put on their coronets. She did not have the ducal leaves but rather the silver circlet with four leaves, but, with her mother-in-law watching, she pretended not to care.

One day she knew she would wear the coronet of a Duchess again.

Now they would feast and intricate dishes were carried in and served to Anne by nobles. Two noble ladies knelt in front of her to serve her as the Royal Book decreed.

While the new Queen sat at the high table, Frances sat at one of the four other tables reserved for the nobility. Commoners were also being fed, and food and wine was being doled out by the kitchen in a generous spirit.

Her father was moving around the tables, leading them in making toasts and congratulating the Queen. Everyone seemed more than happy to attend Anne's coronation, though Frances had seen many argue against the divorce.

They had called Anne nothing more than a whore — though never to her face. Now they were content bowing to her. This was the true power of her uncle the King. He would get what he wanted out of his subjects.

To Frances, it also showed their lack of conviction. If

136

they could be bought and convinced so easily, then she would never be able to trust their word.

～

"Why haven't you asked for a place among Anne's ladies?"

"How could I serve her? You know how I feel about her," Frances said, not keeping the disdain from her voice.

"This is why no rewards come our way."

He was exasperated again. He had lost at cards the night before, and he was ready to find someone to blame for it.

"You should be making yourself useful. Like a good wife."

Frances looked at him without batting an eye. Did he think that would frighten her? That his displeasure would make her run to please him? She was made of sterner stuff than that, though an outward show of defiance would not get her anywhere either.

She thought of the Duchess of Norfolk banished from court up North for being caught writing to the former Queen Catherine. She had not dared to do so either, fearing what would happen. Besides she could think of nothing to comfort Catherine. She would hardly be pleased to read about the new fashions at court or what Anne and the King were doing.

Every day Anne's pregnancy progressed was another day the chance of him reconciling with Catherine was slipping away. They were planning the child's christening already and having declarations drawn up announcing the birth of their son, as every doctor and astrologer were positive Anne was carrying a boy.

Frances would be left in limbo soon as her husband would be accompanying the King on the small progress he was planning to make and the Queen's household would be moving to York Place. Greenwich was to be refurbished and prepared for the Queen's confinement. Cromwell, a new prominent courtier, had been busy making the necessary arrangements. Everything would be done to perfection.

Frances wasn't sure if she should retreat to Bradgate or move with the Queen to York Place. The thought of being underneath Margaret's thumb made her think following Anne would be the lesser of two evils. She could plead ill health and spend most of her time in her rooms or out riding.

She had also purchased a new hawk she could take out while the weather remained so good.

Once her husband returned, perhaps the two of them could travel to Westhorpe and visit her mother.

∾

She had returned from a day of riding exhausted but in high spirits only to find her husband waiting for her in the courtyard. He helped her down and was most tender with her.

"Has the King returned?" she asked.

"He shall be soon enough."

When he did not meet her gaze, she was sure there was something he was hiding from her.

"What is it? You seem like you have something to tell

138

me?" She was pulling off her riding gloves, seeing she had worn a hole in them.

"Come back to our rooms, we shall talk there." He took her hand and pulled her along.

Confused, she let him.

He pushed her down into a chair and then paced the room. She nearly wanted to laugh, but it was clear whatever he had to say was weighing on him. This more than anything made her apprehensive. He had no qualms about lecturing her for something she had done wrong, so she wasn't sure what it could be.

"Your mother has died."

The words cut into the silence of the room. Suddenly, Frances wished she had never heard them. It was as if with his words he had killed her himself.

"But she was going to get better... you must be mistaken, she has not written to me."

He was kneeling before her and in a moment of tenderness held her hands in his. Frances was still too shocked to say anything, but she saw by the expression on his face that he had not been wrong. Nor was this some cruel joke.

"She can't be gone. Why did no one write to me? I am her eldest daughter!" She was suddenly filled with rage.

"I am sure they did not wish to trouble you. But she is dead and your father says we are to see to the funeral arrangements. We shall have to order mourning clothes," he said.

"Mourning clothes?" She thought of the last time she had worn blue, for her brother. Those dresses wouldn't fit her any more. "M-my father. How is he?"

"He is very distraught. The King is as well. They are

already riding back, I was sent ahead to tell you. I am very sorry," he repeated.

"Sorry?" she sniffed. "That won't bring her back. My poor father, she was everything to him. He loved her more than everything and she loved him. How shall he go on?" Now the tears were coming out as the reality of the situation hit her.

"I am here for you. Whatever you need of me."

He seemed so genuine, she threw her arms around his neck and clung to him. It was a long time before she moved. Almost embarrassed, she thanked him for not pulling away.

The news of the Dowager Queen of France spread throughout the court that day. Everyone was sending their condolences and the groom of the wardrobe threw the doors open and took out the mourning clothes.

Queen Anne had sent a short message too. Frances had been ready to throw it into the fire but Henry caught her eye and it stopped her.

"Thank her majesty for her kind message," she said to the man instead, and he bowed and left the room.

"I need to think of what needs to be done. She was a royal Princess, and a Queen."

"Your father will have this all in hand. Take care of yourself. You are her heir."

"My mother's fortune lay in France. There is nothing I want from her."

"You shall have what you are entitled to have." He kissed her brow. "You should rest. I can tell you are tired. We shall speak in the morning."

Exhausted, she complied.

Frances entered the familiar chapel, but she did not walk with confidence though she could have walked up the steps blind. She felt as though she stepped into another world as the heavy smell of incense overcame her. Ahead, lit tapers glowed around the coffin. Beckoning her forward.

She hesitated again. Her feet would not move until she found the strength to continue forward. Finally, she fell before the coffin, clutching at the blue velvet draping over it.

She held on as though for dear life. She knew she should pray or say something. But her throat had closed up. Here lay her mother, and soon she would be entombed in the ground forever. She didn't want to believe that this box is all that remained of her. Never again would she be walking around. Never again would she comment on her failings.

They had cleared the chapel for her to have a few moments alone with her mother, but there was nothing for her to say. There were no more tears to be shed. So she stayed there kneeling in front of the coffin as she used to do at her mother's knees watching her sew or play the lute.

She didn't know how long she remained like that for. A loud creaking noise alerted her that the chapel door had been opened. She did not turn around to see who it was. Instead, she gripped the velvet tighter between her fingers.

This had to be a cruel joke. Her mother would rise up or come out from behind the pulpit and tell them that she had managed to fool them all.

It was Eleanor who came to her side. Her eyes were red

and her face contorted from all the crying and sleepless nights.

"She..."

Frances couldn't listen to what she had to say. She rushed to her feet and left the chapel at a run. She did not wish to hear words of comfort. She did not wish to hear about her mother's last days. She ran to the gardens where she could hide among the trees and rose bushes.

Her mother had always criticized her for not being a true daughter. And it was true. She was a terrible daughter. She had not gone to her mother's side while she was sick and dying. She was not there to care for her. Not there to trade places with her.

She was just not there.

Whatever her other failings, this was something she would never be able to forgive herself for. There was no way she could improve this or make her mother forget.

The priest reassured her always that they would be reunited one day in Heaven. But how could she face her mother? She had died with Eleanor by her side — the perfect daughter to the very end.

She couldn't even begin to confess this fear to anyone. She was so distraught that she jumped when she felt someone's hand on her shoulder.

"Frances, your sister said you ran off," Katherine said, sitting down gingerly beside her on the bench as if she was trying not to spook a wounded animal.

Frances did not look at her. She felt if she did then she would start crying. For here was another perfect angel to remind her of her failings.

"I need to be alone," she croaked.

"You shouldn't be alone at a time like this," Katherine persevered.

"Where is Henry?"

"He left to go back to London. He is going to attend the requiem mass for your mother there. Don't you remember?"

Frances was tired of being spoken to as if she was a little child again. She was a married woman now and she didn't need a girl younger than herself giving her comfort or treating her like an invalid.

"Of course, I remember! I just..." she paused. Unsure of what excuse she was about to give. In truth, she had wished to be with him if only to escape all the concerned faces around her. Even the servants were crying and looking teary-eyed.

"Well let me know if there is anything I can do. It's not good to shut yourself away like this." Katherine stood again.

"Stay, but I don't want to talk about it."

"Alright," Katherine said. "Tell me about your husband. You seem to get along together."

～

For two weeks they alternated staying vigil over her mother's body. She no longer broke down at the sight of it, so Frances thought she was mending. Her husband's return at first gave her some relief. After all, he had sworn to be there for her, but it became abundantly clear that his thoughts were elsewhere than the grief of losing her mother.

He looked at the plates and tapestries like he was an appraiser considering goods at the market place. Frances did not like it one bit, and one morning she told him so too.

"You should leave if you are here only to pick over a dead woman's goods."

"How can you be reproaching me? I have been nothing but kind staying here by your side when I could be at court."

"Why? So, you can catch someone's attention? How? You cannot joust, you aren't half as witty as you think you are. You were only made a Knight of the Bath because you are married to me."

"You are grieving. We shouldn't be fighting."

His voice was cold and she knew she had cut him deeply with her words, but it also angered her to think that he knew what was going on in her mind.

"You just use me for my money."

"If you had some I would gladly take it off of you."

"Go then!" she shouted.

He seemed to hesitate. "I shall and when I return, I hope to find you in better spirits, madam."

He knew how much she hated being called madam.

It was not lost on her that as he left, he pocketed a bracelet she had left on the table. He would likely lose it in a game of cards, but she did not care enough to stop him. She watched him go. Breathing a sigh of relief when she could no longer hear his heavy steps. She shouldn't be fighting with him, but it also made her happy to do so. Not that he didn't deserve it.

He was always running off with his little tag along friends, getting drunk in the park or playing cards well into the night. She was sure they would also sneak away to brothels. She didn't really care — the thought of his infidelity did not bother her. Well she supposed it would if he brought an illegitimate child into her home.

But she knew he would never dream of putting her aside as her uncle had done to his first wife. After all, she was one of the most well-connected ladies in all of England. There was no one better than her with as much royal blood now that Princess Mary was disowned.

He was lucky to be married to her.

She found herself caught up in making arrangements for the funeral. Now that the French delegation had arrived there wouldn't be a reason to delay any further. She felt strongly that her mother should be put to rest.

Katherine was helping her work on what type of cloth would be suitable for the carriage that was to pull the coffin. They had also been discussing the role everyone would play. The household staff would also be heavily involved.

It was then Henry returned, wobbling on his feet and smelling of cheap ale.

"Ah! My wife, there you are." He was grinning from ear to ear.

"Katherine, you should go. My husband is unwell."

Katherine shot her a look, but she did as she was bid.

"What are you doing there, wife?" He was examining the table, picking up the samples of cloth.

"Making arrangements. Put those down," she commanded.

Now his mood turned sour.

"You are always so combative. Do you think you are so special you do not need to respect your husband?" His rant was only interrupted by his hiccupping.

Frances felt a headache coming on, and she took a seat by the fireplace feeling more drained than ever.

"You are quite an unnatural woman... thinking you can order me around," he accused.

She didn't deny it. Not even looking at him, she opened her mouth to speak.

"I don't respect you, as I find you quite beneath me by your inferior birth, rank and behavior."

He reached for the first object he could and flung it hard towards the fire.

"You foul b—"

The glare she turned on her husband stopped him in his tracks. He staggered a moment later and grabbed onto the table to steady himself.

Frances's attention moved to the shattered glass before the fireplace. Another precious heirloom lost. She focused on the glass to keep her own anger in check. There was no point arguing with him when he was like this. Her husband was a drunk and an imbecile, but mostly he was a disappointed man who clung to his dreams.

"I'll send you away from court. Yes, that's what I'll do."

"And what will that achieve?" She couldn't help herself from lashing out at him.

"I won't have to see your simpering face and be reminded of your failure to procure me a position on the King's council."

"Go then and see what you can accomplish on your own. I will place a bet that it won't be much." Her smile was icy as she pulled out a gold coin from her purse.

He was gone without another word.

She was left alone again. Frances was still staring at the

broken glass, knowing she should call someone in to clean up. Then she looked at the intact glass on her side table still filled with wine. Without thinking she picked it up flinging it at the fire place where it joined its twin on the floor.

She watched the shattered pieces fall to the floor with grim satisfaction.

❧

Katherine made no mention of Henry's disappearance. There was no time for anyone to notice anyways.

But he surprised her by returning on the day of the funeral to walk at her side as they walked to the abbey at Bury St Edmunds.

More than a hundred torch bearers led the congregation, followed by a priest, knights, nobles and officers of her household. The carriage bearing her mother's coffin with an effigy of her lying on top holding a scepter to represent her former rank as a crowned Queen. Standard-bearers flanked the carriage along with several of her father's yeomen, all carrying lit tapers.

Frances walked directly behind the carriage, a dark veil over her face. Her brother walked on one side and her husband on the other. Often his hand would make its way into hers, giving her reassuring squeezes along the way.

Her half-sisters had also made an appearance. It had been many years since she had seen them. She knew they had been close to her mother, who had been kind enough to raise them herself, but their excessive crying and wailing was grating on her nerves. Eleanor was also behind her and they appeared to be of one mind in regards to their half-sisters.

Eleanor looked just as tense as Frances was.

For sixteen miles they walked, local people who knew her mother joined them to pay their respects from all over the county. Frances looked at the enormous crowd behind her. She wondered if she could ever inspire this much adoration and love.

It was afternoon by the time the coffin was placed at the altar. Priests and others would wait overnight with her body.

The next day the mass was said early in the morning. Both Frances and Eleanor were now acting as the pall-bearers.

Each in turn, they placed the cloth of gold on top of their mother's coffin as the Abbot directed them to do and they returned to their seats. But they had barely sat down in their seats when Frances saw to her horror that their half-sisters had pushed their way to the front. Each also had a cloth of gold in their hands.

She could hardly yell out to stop them. She looked left to right and saw that Eleanor was equally affronted. Katherine was gaping at the rudeness. Henry was frowning.

Eleanor gripped her hand tightly before saying, "I cannot watch. Let's go."

They did not stay to see the household officers breaking their staff of office over her grave or to distribute food to the poor.

"I will make sure they get nothing of hers. They are not welcome here anymore." Frances promised the crying Eleanor back in their rooms.

"Father won't like that."

"Father isn't here, and, by the time he can reverse the order, it'll be too late anyways," she said firmly.

It was true she was now the eldest and in charge of the household until her father came to relieve her of duty. She wondered if perhaps she would be given Westhorpe. Her father would surely have no use for it now.

~

They stayed in seclusion for another week before her father arrived with half his retinue of household staff behind him. Frances went out to the stable yard to be the first to greet him. He hugged her tightly in an uncharacteristic show of affection.

"Was it all done as she wished?"

Frances spared him the details but nodded.

"Shall you be leaving soon?" he asked, walking inside the open doors.

Frances struggled to keep pace with his steps.

"Leaving where?"

"I am closing down Westhorpe."

"But why?" Frances saw her dreams of staying here vanish.

"It is expensive keeping this household open and as you know I am in a great amount of debt. We won't have your mother's dower payments from France anymore."

"Surely..."

"Why don't you summon your mother's servants to the great hall?"

She did as he bid her and watched as one by one he

thanked them for their service, paying them a fee and dismissed them. Some of these people she had seen all her life. It shocked her to see them being let go now. In fact, she too was being encouraged to leave. Her father seemed set on getting rid of anything of her mother's.

Mary's will was read out and her possessions doled out. Frances was left with a few jewels and Eleanor the same including the lute given to her by the French King. All in all, there was very little to be distributed. Her clothing was shared among her daughters, but her father held back much of the jewels and finery. With a hapless shrug he said he needed them to pay off the creditors.

Seeing as her father was so keen to leave Westhorpe, Frances packed up her own things and small household and decided to head back to London.

Henry had gone ahead and she wrote to him that she would meet him in a few days. She thought perhaps she would go to Bradgate, but she was not welcome there either. Her mother-in-law commanded that she go to London to be there to attend the birth of the King's new baby and heir.

She was too tired to argue now.

~

At the end of August, the Queen had gone into confinement not with the grace of a Queen but with the drama of a commoner fishwife. Frances heard from her husband how she had railed at the King to be faithful only to have him yell back that she should endure as her betters had done. Frances had learned from her doctors that she was expecting too. It was a blessing for her to conceive so early in their marriage.

"Did he really say that?" Frances was gloating as she imagined what Anne Boleyn must have looked like when he said this to her.

"Yes. I am sure if she was not with child he would have railed at her some more."

"She never knew how to behave with proper decorum."

He gave her a look that seemed to say she didn't always behave properly either, but he knew better than to argue with her now.

Their tempestuous relationship had cooled into an amicable partnership. They learned to avoid getting on each other's nerves and decided it would be better to fight with others than with each other. She overlooked his drinking and he overlooked the fact she had not been able to win for him the position in court that he craved.

Or they tried to.

They had another reason to learn to work together.

"We have to find a way to get your mother to leave Bradgate. You are old enough now to be settled into your own estate. She is not a good guardian and you have proven yourself more than capable."

"You tell her that then," he said.

"Perhaps it is not her I need to tell." She arranged her hair underneath her headdress. "Leave it to me then. For I swear to you I shall have my child born in its own house."

"Our child," he reminded her, placing a hand over the growing bump.

"You know what I meant." She shoved his hand away but smiled.

"I heard your father has sold Westhorpe."

"Along with a lot of his jewels. The King has even forgiven him part of his debt to the crown, but there are others who aren't so forgiving," she said. It was by now an old topic of discussion between them. Her father though being a Duke was at risk of becoming destitute. Without the friendship of the King, he would have already been out on the streets.

The trouble was, they relied on her father to supplement their meager allowance from his mother, but now that he had become so unreliable, Frances was desperate to find other means of income. If only she had been able to stomach serving the Boleyn Queen. But Anne would never shower her with favors even if she had bowed and scraped.

So at least she had her dignity.

They were certain the Marquess and Marchioness of Dorset would find the money somehow.

With the Queen locked up in her rooms, the King was free to spend his time with other ladies. He often rode out with Madge Shelton and several other ladies. They all vied for his attention for unsavory reasons, but Frances wished to gain his ear for a personal matter. It was about time she benefited from being part of the royal family.

She finally got her chance while they were out riding one day. He had arranged for a picnic in the forest where he gorged himself as usual. She had brought a present for him that he would enjoy, and perhaps it would soften him up to her.

He spotted her out of the corner of his eye hanging back but clearly waiting to speak to him.

"Lady Grey! Come here."

"Your Grace." She stepped forward, curtseying quickly.

"What is that you are hiding behind your back?"

She smiled at her obese uncle who had once been so handsome. "I brought something from home for you. I knew you might enjoy it."

"Well..." he said expectantly.

She showed him the jar of preserves she had been hiding. "This is the last of my mother's preserves. I know how much you liked it and that she would often send you some for Christmas. I thought it would be fitting for you to have the last."

He blinked. Apparently, he was not very pleased to be reminded of his loss, but he accepted the gift.

"That was very thoughtful of you niece." He wiped away a dribble of sauce from his chin with a napkin. "Why do I not see you in my wife's rooms?"

Frances had not been expecting this question. "I have been unwell, sire. It is always an honor to serve in her rooms."

He laughed and the courtiers around him laughed nervously as well.

"Perhaps it is to your benefit that you do not spend time in her rooms." He pointed a finger at her. "You know how a wife should behave don't you?"

"Y-yes, sire."

"Where's your husband?" He looked around for him.

"Back at the palace. His horse went lame, and he could not join the hunt."

"Well, I remember you on your wedding day. You are a sweet girl. Thank you for your gift. Tell your husband to borrow horses from my own stables next time we go hunting. You two lovebirds shouldn't be apart."

He laughed at some private joke, she did not quite understand. What she did understand was that she was dismissed for now. She had won little except to remind the King of her existence and to ensure her husband would not be without a horse from now on.

Still she did not give up. It wasn't until that evening when she was sitting at the ladies table that she was inspired by Cromwell's appearance at the King's side. It was he who was now chief advisor to the King. He seemed to possess some magical power of climbing the social ranks.

If rumors were to be believed, he was some butcher's son or the son of a blacksmith, something like that. But it was his job as a lawyer that inspired her.

They had the option of taking his mother to court over the low allowance she was giving them. They could force her hand, and Henry had friends in the King's council. Surely, they would take his side. They wouldn't like to see a greedy woman stealing from her son and heir.

Besides, Henry was distantly related to the King himself — should he not get what he was owed?

That night Henry was pleased by her suggestion but apprehensive.

"She's my mother. How could I drag her name through the mud in public like that?"

"You are the one who always complains about her," she pointed out.

"Yes... but this is altogether different."

Frances was getting exasperated. "She is leaving us destitute. If she was a loving mother she would give you what you deserve. You need to get justice. It would be nothing more than what you are entitled to as the Marquess of Dorset."

He faltered, running a hand through his hair. "Perhaps..."

"It is the only way."

"I shall write to her again and use such language, she will know that she has to comply."

"Fine but I am going to see what you write." Seeing his frown at her tone she added more sweetly, "If it would please you."

~

Frances was in her rooms reading over her husband's letter when Katherine entered. She was unannounced and unaccompanied. She looked pale and Frances wondered if she was sick.

They had not seen much of each other since her mother's funeral. Truth be told, she had not inquired about where she would go or what would happen to her. It was with some shock that she appeared a week ago at court.

"Katherine! What a pleasant surprise. I was just going over some papers. Are you unwell? I cannot take any risks." A hand went to her belly.

Katherine shook her head. "Can I sit?"

Frances was confused but decided to amuse her friend and nodded.

"You have something on your mind clearly. Well out with it."

"Now that I've come here I cannot say!" She groaned. "I don't know how to begin."

"This is good news?"

"I believe so."

"Then tell me. Has some young man written you a poem?" She teased, only to see her friend go whiter still.

"Something like that. I am getting married." Immediately after saying this, she started rambling and Frances had to stop her.

"What?"

"I'm getting married."

"But you are engaged to my brother. You cannot break the betrothal."

"It is already done."

"My father would never allo..." She paused. "Who are you marrying?"

"Him."

"Who's him?" Frances felt the growing apprehension rise in her belly. She knew who she was referring to, but she refused to believe it.

"Your father, the Duke of Suffolk. The King gave his blessing. He told me this morning. We are to wed Sunday."

Frances was laughing so hard she thought her stomacher would burst open.

"You cannot be serious. Why would he marry you? He wouldn't marry you. My mother was just recently buried. This is a cruel joke."

Katherine shook her head. She had grown still and serious.

"I am marrying him."

"He could never love you. He is old and you are too

young. You must have misunderstood. I don't want to discuss this any further."

"I am marrying him," she repeated this time with more conviction.

"You cannot..." Frances felt her face redden. "Have you no heart? Think of what it would do to my mother if she knew. How could you betray her like that? You could never take her place."

"This is a good marriage for me. I loved your mother but she is gone now. You are just unhappy that I will have a higher position than you. Don't pretend like that is the only reason you don't want me to marry him. You knew your father would have to marry again. You just don't want to see me rise from my station," she accused.

"I—" The point hit home and made her stutter. Katherine kept on going.

"You have always put me down. You were always so worried about yourself and what you could and couldn't do. You hated anyone who might outshine you. You are petty and selfish. Don't deny it!" Katherine's chest was rising fast.

Frances finally found her tongue, though the rest of her body had tensed.

"He's marrying you for your money. He will never care for you as he cared for my mother. You are nothing. You were lucky to be taken in by us. You were lucky I bothered to befriend you!"

"It will still be a stronger foundation than what you have in your marriage. Before you point fingers at me, think of your own husband. Did he not marry you to get closer to the crown? He's just as ambitious as any of us. Before you think I was lucky, know that I had to put up with you for years. You don't have a kind bone in your body. You lost your mother, but I was taken away from mine. I have no control over where I go and who I marry. Can you think beyond yourself for a second?" Katherine was panting now. "I cannot wait to see you walk behind me as we go into dinner. You will have to call me mother. How do you feel about that?"

Frances wanted to throw something but there was nothing on hand for her to do so. She suppressed her desire to leap at Katherine and begin tearing out her hair.

Katherine had taken a deep breath and seemed to try to be collecting herself.

"I apologize. I came here to tell you, not to ask for your permission. I thought perhaps as my friend you would be supportive or at least understanding. This is a good match for me, even if you think it is less than ideal. It is true he is much older than me, but I don't have the luxury to choose exactly."

Her words might have made sense to her if she was of a different frame of mind, but all she was seeing was red. Was her mother watching them from heaven? What would she think of all of this? She had risked everything when she had married Charles Brandon. Now her love was forgotten and her memory insulted.

"You are no friend of mine. I never want to see you again!"

Katherine left and Frances remained in her seat for quite some time, unable to process what had happened. It felt as though someone had knocked the air out of her lungs. Her head was swimming with thoughts. This wedding could not happen. Her father would never go through with it.

She remembered how everyone said that her parents were a love match, but if this was what love was then she did not want it. She had no need for such a fickle thing.

Henry found her pacing the length of the room, her face twisted in contempt. She could articulate what happened as she couldn't even believe it herself.

"At least he will be able to draw from her inheritance now."

She didn't appreciate the silver-lining.

"I must leave court. I cannot stay here. Your mother has to leave Bradgate."

"Don't be rash."

"I'm not. I am thinking of the health of our child and staying here would only aggravate me."

He held her in his arms, the tight grip comforting her as she began sobbing into his shoulder.

～

On the day of her father's wedding, the Queen had also gone into labor. Frances could not leave now. While the Queen toiled in her chambers, her father was saying his vows with Katherine. Frances had refused to attend and refused to accept any of her father's letters and messages, though she suspected Henry took them on her behalf so they wouldn't have a falling out with him.

Everyone was waiting on tenterhooks to see if Anne's child would be a boy or a girl.

Frances found herself in her uncle's chamber, watching

from the sidelines as he ate and drank while playing cards. Her husband was playing too and was trying his best not to appear as though he cared about every lost coin. It was obvious he was losing money rather than gaining it.

They were prepared to play well into the night. No one would sleep until the baby was born. Luckily, they did not have to wait long. In the afternoon, Mary Boleyn came to the King's rooms.

She looked exhausted but everyone immediately saw that she did not look triumphant either.

"The Queen has been delivered of a healthy baby girl, your grace," she said, curtseying to him. "You have a daughter."

His disappointment was clear to everyone, but he wasn't so ungracious that he said anything now in public.

"And the Queen is well?"

"Yes, she is well and resting now, sire." Mary curtseyed again, but her eyes wandered to her uncle, the Duke of Norfolk.

Frances followed her gaze and saw that he too was trying his best to hide his disappointment.

The Boleyns were quick to rally and everyone congratulated the King. Many claimed that since they were so fertile, a brother would follow shortly. But Frances wondered if the calculating Duke was already making a contingency plan. It was no secret that he had a falling out with Anne.

❧

Anne was still confined to her rooms waiting until she could be churched and re-enter court life. Frances saw an opportunity now to approach her uncle, the King, for help with her mother-in-law. She convinced Henry to walk with her, and she led him down to the archery butts, knowing the King was shooting today with some of his friends.

Upon seeing the Yeomen of the Guard, Henry looked down at her with a quizzical look. She merely smiled up at him and lead him closer to the gathered nobles.

They did not make their presence known as the King was pulling back the string of his bow. His eyes fixed on the target ahead.

He breathed in, and then released the arrow. It flew true and sunk into the center of the target.

"Bravo!" Frances shouted louder than the others and applauded.

When the King turned around to see who had shouted, she curtseyed low, her hand to her mouth as though she was embarrassed she had shouted so loudly.

"Ah, Lady Grey, have you come to join our little celebration?"

She rose from her curtsey. Seeing he was in a jovial mood today, she approached.

"My husband and I were just taking a stroll for some fresh air."

"Would he care to join me at a little friendly competition?"

Frances interrupted before her husband could agree. "I fear he doesn't shoot half as well as you do, your grace. It would be a poor competition. He was just telling me about his wonderful family home of Bradgate. How I dearly wish I could see it."

"Why should you not see it?" The King handed his bow

to one of his companions and asked for his crossbow to be brought to him.

"I would rather not say." Frances looked abashed.

"Speak up."

"His mother holds control of the house and refuses to allow us to live in it properly as man and wife. I am ashamed to admit this..."

"Has your father not spoken to her?"

"She is a headstrong woman. Thinking she knows best—"

"Would she dare refuse the command of the King?" The King, likely thinking of Anne Boleyn's tempers, was incensed.

"I daresay she would not." Frances beamed at her uncle.

"Cromwell, make sure you make my displeasure known to—" He looked down at Frances who named her mother-in-law.

"Margaret Wotton, your majesty."

The darkly clad man nodded. "I shall see it is done."

She kissed her uncle's hand in thanks and retreated back to her husband's side.

Henry was incredulous.

"You have succeeded?"

"At the very least, Bradgate shall be ours. You must continue to press your case with the King's council."

"I shall, I promise."

∼

The new Princess was to be christened in a grand ceremony at the Church of the Observant Friars.

Pleading ill health, Frances retired to Bradgate a day later. There was no need to stay behind for the baby's christening. She also knew that her mother-in-law had been named as a Godmother to the baby, so she would be leaving Bradgate.

She had told Margaret to move to the second-best rooms, but she doubted she had listened. She wasn't above strong-arming her to get what she wanted.

$\sim$

Frances arrived at Bradgate to see that her mother-in-law had indeed vacated the best rooms for her. Her own steward and chamberlain saw that the keys of the house and the account books were transferred to her. She showed no weakness and merely demanded what she wanted, rather than asking.

She found the linen in the rooms were not to her liking and sent for the yeoman of her chamber to order new ones. She picked hues of blues to adorn her rooms and even ordered new furniture.

Margaret's seething disapproval was felt each and every day, but Frances strove to ignore her. Margaret had no power to stop her. The King had agreed her husband should have Bradgate back in his keeping. Henry's mother could not argue with the King and found she no longer held tight control of the purse strings. She relinquished control begrudgingly, and it was often reported to Frances that Margaret had instructed the servants to withhold information.

Having enough, Frances marched down the halls to the

east wing, followed by two of her ladies. She found Margaret writing at her desk.

"Will you please tell me why you have refused to give my usher the inventory of the household goods?"

"I have misplaced the papers. There was no reason for you to barge in here like this."

"This is my house and you stay here at my pleasure." Frances put a hand to her belly.

"It was once mine. If you are so determined to take control of the reins and manage this household then I suggest you tell your people to make an inventory themselves. Since I am to be retired, I shall enjoy myself."

Frances regarded her coolly. "Of course, I would not wish to trouble you. It might be better for you to retire to one of Henry's country houses. Perhaps in Lincolnshire."

"This is my home." Margaret was on her feet, faster than it seemed possible.

"I do hope we can work together and come to an accord. I am mistress here now. Bradgate is mine whether you like it or not. You may consider it your home, but it is not yours any longer. Perhaps if you had been kinder..." She left the end of the sentence hanging in the air.

Margaret's chest was visibly rising in and out with each breath she took as she fought to restrain herself.

The inventory appeared miraculously the next day in the hands of her usher. Frances was pleased with herself. She shouldn't let herself be bullied by those of lesser birth.

~

By the time she was six months along, her mother-in-law had packed up her things and moved to her house in Croydon. Now the uncontested mistress of Bradgate, she relished the power of her authority.

Often, she wished she was able to ride into the town Leicester. Like her mother before her, she too enjoyed performing ceremonial tasks such as awarding prizes at the fair. But due to her condition, she was confined to a litter, making such journeys tiresome.

Then a happy surprise greeted her one morning.

A messenger from her husband sent news that he was to arrive at Bradgate with a retinue of friends. He also sent a gift. Frances threw back the cloth covering her gift to reveal a cage. Inside was a little fledgling bird.

"Oh!" she exclaimed as she put her fingers through the grate. The little creature was not fully formed but still had tufts of white fluff on its body.

"It is a peregrine falcon purchased for you by your husband." The messenger handed her a sealed note.

She ripped the seal and read.

He wrote that he knew how she must be missing going out hunting every day and hoped that the distraction of training her own bird from such a young age would prove a suitable replacement. He wished her well and told her to ask the falconer for anything she might need.

She looked at the little creature again. Its dark eyes fixed on her. She felt a blooming appreciation for her husband. He had never been so thoughtful before. It nearly made her want to cry.

"Take the bird to the mews. I shall come down shortly after I have changed."

Her husband arrived with a troupe of fifty men accompanying them. It would have been hard for Frances to miss his encroaching arrival as all the horses were kicking up dust on the road. She had arranged for rooms to be prepared with her chamberlain and had the kitchens working around the clock to ensure she had enough food to feed them all.

Frances was surprised by the number of friends her husband seemed to have. She had always looked down on him and teased him about his lack of position, but it was evident she had been mistaken.

Dressed in a new gown of red velvet, she greeted her husband as he jumped from his horse in the stable yard.

"You look well, Lady Grey." He placed a chaste kiss on her lips. Her growing belly between them. "And how is my son doing in there?" He whispered this last part so only she could hear.

"He is growing strong. I feel him moving sometimes." She returned his smile, happy to see his joy at seeing her again.

They enjoyed three days of feasting. Frances could not even imagine the drain on their estate but she did not care. She enjoyed sitting beside Henry in the great hall. Each dish was brought in to a flourish of trumpets. Mutton in gravy, swans, roasted pheasant filled their bellies until they felt they were going to burst.

During the day, the men rode out hunting the rich forests surrounding Bradgate. When they returned they would play cards and place bets on the winners. On the second day, they arranged for a cock fight in the courtyard outside. Frances found her stomach go queasy at the sight of blood, and she had to look away.

She found herself laughing and enjoying herself more than ever. Her eyes constantly searched for her husband, and she found that she was beginning to miss him when he was not by her side. As any decent husband, he did not lie with her at night, but he still brought her a warm jug of spiced wine and they drank it together and spoke of their plans for the day ahead.

Only their chaplain, James Haddon, did not approve of their revelry. He used such forceful language to Frances that she had been tempted to yell back at him.

"We encourage the servants not to gamble. In fact, we have forbidden them to do so. What we do with our friends in our private rooms is not for you to judge. We confess to you our sins. But gambling is the way of our world. What fun would it be if there were no stakes?" Frances argued.

Her chaplain did not seem impressed, but he also sensed her anger and did not press the matter any further.

As the days of her encroaching confinement began nearing, she clung to her husband for companionship. She did not admit to him that she was scared and found his boisterous spirit heartening, but he seemed to appreciate having a doting wife.

When she was not with him, she was training her bird with the falconer. They used lures of meat to get the little bird to hop from one perch to another to get its food. Slowly, it would learn to fly to its quarry and return to her gloved hands.

Frances couldn't wait to be free to do the same.

Her son was born in March.

He had come easily into the world, but she could tell there was something wrong. No one dared say anything to her, but she was not so blind that she couldn't tell he was small and, though he fed well, he did not seem to be gaining weight.

She found she couldn't bear to hold him for long, nor did she find his little smiles adorable.

She was proud to have provided her husband with a son and heir, something Queen Anne had failed to do, but she did not seem to get the joy that other mothers got at the sight of their children. She found she could forgive her own mother's coldness towards her. Children, especially at this age, were more of a nuisance, and her son had wreaked havoc on her body.

Her once flat stomach now felt flabby and malformed.

It was Henry who had turned into a doting father overnight. She often found him in their son's nursery, and she knew he visited every night when he wasn't at court.

By the council's decree, his mother had finally been forced to hand over all the lands she was holding on behalf of her son, and her wardship was stripped away. They had argued before the King's council and her son had won. They looked at Henry with a new son in his cradle and sided with him just as Frances knew they would. Frances only cared that Bradgate was now firmly in her keeping.

Bradgate had become her refuge from the world outside.

Her father had been forced to relinquish his holdings on

many of her childhood homes, and though he had been gifted lands in Lincolnshire, she had never visited them yet. She had not seen Katherine since that fateful day, though she often thought of her which only ended up filling her with a rage that filled her to her core.

Her father, she could forgive. He was always pragmatic and had been desperate for money. He was also in need of an heir.

Her brother had died just weeks ago and their family was plunged into mourning. She had been unable to attend the funeral as she was in the last months of her pregnancy, but it saddened her to think that her mother's heir wouldn't inherit her father's lands.

Of course, it didn't surprise her to hear that Katherine was now pregnant. She seemed to get everything she wanted.

Eleanor was settled down to married life as well, and they exchanged letters occasionally. Eleanor had not had the bad falling out with Katherine that she had and Frances knew they saw each other often. This made her feel equally betrayed by her sister.

As the weather turned warm, she looked forward to the freedom of being able to ride out and hunt again.

In the summer, they also had plans to renovate and build a bear pit and jousting lists. She would turn Bradgate into a modern palace for herself.

She had no need of London.

She had no need of anyone.

PART II

— NINE YEARS LATER —

CHAPTER FIVE

1543

"You would spoil our children," Frances accused her husband.

"No, I wish to see them raised properly. A proper education is admirable to have. With their good breeding, they should be as talented as the Lady Mary — if not more so," he said.

She eyed him suspiciously. "I suppose if you think we can spare the expense. I know it is fashionable for the ladies of the court to be highly educated now."

"Good." He patted her knee. "I was sure you would see my way."

She sighed, not wishing to hide the exasperation in her voice. "Learning languages was enough education for me."

"Frances, I have great plans for our daughters."

"And our sons?" she snapped.

"And them when they come as God will surely grant them to us," he spoke more tenderly to her now. "We are still young. You needn't concern yourself."

She nodded but fixed her gaze on her hands in her lap. She thought of Queen Catherine who had been put aside for not bearing her husband a male heir. She wondered if Henry would do the same to her.

Her thoughts were elsewhere as he pulled her towards him trailing kisses up her neck in a gesture of loving devotion.

Could she trust him not to put her aside? She tried not to think of the little coffins buried behind the church. They were a reminder of both her failure and the cruelty dealt out to her in droves by fate.

As if sensing her temper giving way to despair, her husband stopped. A moment later he pressed a cup of wine into her hands.

"Shall we play some cards instead?"

She took a sip of wine and nodded, the dark thoughts melting away just as quickly as they had formed.

❦

Frances left Bradgate in good spirits. She was heading for London to join the May Day celebrations. The sun shone brightly overhead, promising an easy journey.

Her newest addition to her household, Adrian Stokes, her Master of Horse, accompanied her. He proved to be jovial company on the journey. They spoke at length about the newest greyhounds he had purchased to breed for her.

After her previous Master of Horse had died of the

sweating sickness, her husband had recommended him, knowing he had a knack for horses. Since then, he had become invaluable to her.

Her steward and two gentlemen ushers rode just behind her while the majority of her household followed after them. She now had the full retinue of a Marchioness.

She was no longer a little girl fighting to gain control.

Following in the footsteps of her mother before her, she had taken a great interest in the lands and villages surrounding Bradgate, making sure to support the local pageants anyway she could.

"We shall have to get Jane a new pony. She will be old enough to join the hunt."

"I don't think she would enjoy that very much," he said apologetically.

"Nonsense, she enjoys studying and God knows she's a brilliant girl, but there's more to life than books," Frances said.

Her thoughts turned to the six-year-old in her nursery who day by day proved how intelligent she was. She should have been filled with pride, but she found she could not relate to and understand this daughter of hers.

She tried to be a good mother but felt she was failing daily somehow.

She had not doted on her children as others had done. During their infancy, she tended to avoid them. The loss of her son had retaught her how fragile children were. Many lived fleeting lives and she could not bring herself to grow too attached.

It did not help that she was left feeling as though her husband's attention was waning. He was caught up in the

New Learning, always reading or writing something. When he wasn't doing that, he was seeing to their children. He took great care to appoint only the very best tutors.

It felt like a reproach to her whenever she found him and Jane sequestered together with books in his study. She knew they were discussing theology and philosophy. She had tried joining them once but found she had dozed off when Jane had nudged her to stop her from snoring.

She wanted him to come riding with her as they used to do, but he had less and less time for her.

She looked at Jane with her seemingly magical power for holding his interest and couldn't help but feel a twang of jealousy. It made her feel ridiculous. Her daughter repre-sented the future and for that Henry adored Jane. He looked at Jane as though he expected her to conquer the world. Frances knew that Henry cherished her and respected her as his wife but he did not love her like the troubadour in poems.

Frances wanted to be adored. She deserved it.

Her whole life, no one looked at her with that sort of love. Her father, though kind, had been solely focused on her mother. As for her mother, she never won her mother's approval though she struggled for it daily. Even her own friends had the tendency to betray her.

When her party arrived at Greenwich, she headed for Lady Mary's rooms. There was no Queen on the throne at the moment, and now the daughter of the King's first wife, Catherine of Aragon, was the leading woman of the court.

It was hard to believe in the last nine years she had seen four Queens come and go.

It had been a relief to see Anne Boleyn brought so low,

but her beheading still chilled Frances. To think that the King could be so cruel.

She embraced Lady Mary with a tenderness she had not shown her own children. They had grown up together, and Frances had borne witness to her fall from grace and her revival. There was now a royal Prince growing up at Hertford and Mary's father, the King, had made peace with his daughter.

For her part, Lady Mary never forgot how they spent days walking by the Thames in her youth and then later the letters Frances had helped her pass along in secret to her exiled mother.

That seemed so long ago.

She caught sight of Catherine Parr nearby and greeted her friend with a smile.

"You seem well," she said, taking a seat beside her.

"I had been troubled, but I have made up my mind with God's guidance."

Frances was intrigued. "What is it that has been troubling you?"

Catherine seemed unsure if she should confide in her but decided to tell her.

"The King has been most attentive to me and kind. He has proposed and I have accepted him," she whispered into her ear.

"When?" Frances was breathless. Part of her couldn't believe there would be another Queen! The third Queen Catherine to sit on the throne beside her uncle. The other part of her was happy to see her friend elevated so highly. Though she struggled with herself to try to suppress the jealousy at the thought of what power she would hold.

"The plans are being made already. Not long now, the King says sometime in July."

"Congratulations." Frances looked to Mary who was talking to Lady Margaret Douglas. "Is Lady Mary pleased?"

"I am sure she has her reservations, but she has not voiced them. I think I shall show her I shall be a good guardian to her, and I hope a good mother to her younger siblings."

Of course, how could Mary dare to speak up against her father's wishes?

"I am sure you will be." Thinking it would take a strong woman to step into the shoes of five previous wives.

Frances had seen how strong Catherine could be. She had been left alone by her previous husband as her castle was laid siege by the rebellious Northerners in Lincolnshire. Now a widow for the second time in her life, Catherine was sure to plow ahead.

❧

It was as the King had said, and their wedding took place on July 12th.

Frances helped her prepare for her wedding day, dressing her in the cream silk gown sent up to her by the King. It was a simple ceremony held in the Queen's Privy Closet at Hampton Court.

Lady Anne Herbert, the Queen's sister, was all smiles. Her shoulders pushed back, strutting around as proudly as any peacock, happy with her sister's rise to power.

Frances looked to her husband with a knowing smile. They had seen many families rise and fall with the marriage of a kinswoman to the King. Hopefully, Catherine would fare better, as there were no guarantees of the King's favor.

She was doing her best to ignore a certain someone in the room. Katherine Willoughby, the Duchess of Suffolk, was there. She was standing beside Lady Elizabeth while Frances had chosen to stand to the left of the other sister Mary to act as a barrier.

For years, she had done her best to ignore and avoid talking to Katherine. There had been the odd letter to her father, congratulating him on the birth of his two sons by her and random family news. Her own failure to produce a son weighed heavily on her. She somehow felt Katherine was responsible. Not only had she robbed her mother's place, but she had continued to thrive where she had failed.

It irked Frances that she was popular at court, known for her beauty and wit. She was held up as an example of the perfect wife and Frances couldn't help but hate her even more for it.

Following the fashion, Katherine had taken up with the New Faith and was known to be a reformer. Frances's father, Charles, had even let Katherine name her dog Gardiner. An insult to the Bishop who was secretly thought to be a papist.

They dined after the ceremony. A feast that went on for hours as the King kept calling in for more and more food. Frances, well accustomed to his large feasts, paced herself as she sat beside her husband.

"I think you shall be pleased to hear that the King is working on an act of succession to put before Parliament," Henry murmured to her.

"Oh?" She sat up straighter in her seat and leaned closer to him.

"No one knows anything for sure, but I heard rumors that your aunt Margaret has been overlooked, which means..."

"Me..." Frances had to quickly close her mouth realizing she was gaping like some fool.

"It is very likely the King has honored you," he said, careful with his choice of words in case anyone could overhear.

"Us." She touched his hand. Her mind on the glory of being named officially to the succession.

A plate of thin slices of beef rolled to resemble larks was put before them. Another server drizzled thick gravy over them. Her mouth watered at the rich smell, and, finding her appetite again, she served herself a generous portion.

She did not have to wait long to have her position in the succession confirmed. By Act of Parliament, she was now officially fourth in line for the throne. The news filled her with a sensation of elation she had never felt before. A world of opportunity seemed to have opened before her. She looked to her husband to see the pride evident on his face.

They were so close to the power and privilege they had only dreamed of.

"We shall have to arrange a brilliant marriage for Jane," he mused out loud, in the privacy of their room. "If anything should happen, she could be in line for the throne."

"There are many people before her," Frances said, not

to mention herself but she did not say this. "And we shall have a son. I know we will."

He patted her on the head as if she was a child herself. He wasn't thinking of her. He didn't picture her on the throne. Had she not shown him how strong she was?

And just like that, her life was slipping away from her again, and she wasn't sure how to stop it.

She poured herself some wine.

Letting the drink dull her senses until she was overcome with a feeling of giddiness.

Then an idea struck her to distract her. Jane could come to court and serve the Queen. It was time she learned how to serve her family and do her duty. She would mention this to him later.

～

Her husband's lackluster response might have been a disappointment, but there was no mistaking the difference in the way people were treating her. Suddenly, many were approaching her. Ready to smile and laugh with her, inviting her to gamble or join them in a game.

She was being treated with a different sort of deference. The Spanish and French Ambassadors, who had not spared her much thought, now found the time to say good morning to her.

She laid down in bed at night with a satisfied sigh, knowing she was now someone special.

Frances was no fool though, she knew that the closer she got to the throne, the more enemies she was making. The Seymour brothers, uncles to the young Prince and heir apparent, treated her coolly now as if they feared she might usurp their power.

None of the King's daughters were married and there were no plans for their marriage. They could not produce male heirs to inherit. But she was married, she proved she was fertile, and, though God had taken away her child, she was still young and sure to inherit.

If anything were to happen to the sickly Prince — God forbid — who's to say the people wouldn't look to her. After all, the King's daughters were still illegitimate. Their claim on the throne would always be questioned.

Frances was of course sorry for Princess Mary, but she would treat her kindly if she was put on the throne instead of her. She would be generous. Thoughts of her graciousness filled her with a special pride.

It was Henry who was worried about the animosity of the Seymour brothers.

"They aren't to be trifled with," he cautioned her. "If the Prince were to still be in his minority when he comes to his throne, then they would have command of him. They might see us as a threat and trust me when I tell you that they won't balk at removing those they see as enemies."

She knew he was referring to the Boleyns. They had managed to topple the once powerful family.

"They didn't do it alone," she reminded him. "Besides, we have neither position nor power at court." Though she silently added *yet* in her mind.

"No, but they might ensure we never get it either."

She laughed at the deep worry on his face and kissed his cheek. "Husband, don't fret over nothing."

"If they whisper to the King..."

182

"There is nothing they can say." She kissed him again. Hushing him as she would a child. She kissed him again until she saw the worry melt from his face.

"Come, I don't think we are hunting until later and it has been days since we last slept together." She pulled him towards their bed.

If only she could give him a son, then their position would be cemented.

~

She bit into a roasted apple, savoring each bite before reaching for some gingerbread. She had a hankering for sweets and hoped she was right about the cause.

It was late by the time she made her way to the Queen's rooms. The group of ladies was listening intently to a lecturer from Cambridge. She curtseyed to the Queen's back and took a seat silently beside Lady Mary so as not to interrupt the speaker.

She was surprised her Catholic cousin was attending, but perhaps she did not wish to antagonize her new step-mother who had thus far been more than kind to her.

She found her mind slipping as he droned on, reading from the work of Erasmus, interpreting his words. He made his case and then the Queen began debating with him, challenging his views and inviting her other ladies to do so too.

Frances never had much to add, though she found it strange to be so absorbed in learning. She thought of Anne Boleyn's court of debauchery and excitement, then the childish antics of Katherine Howard. This was more of a University than a court, though some of the most beautiful and powerful women were here, not serious theologians.

In the corner, the Bishop of Chichester was listening with interest to the Queen speaking. His face all but shouting his encouragement. Perhaps Catherine could not see, but Frances was not blind to his attempts to push her further down the path of reform.

Her husband warned her of Gardiner's displeasure at discovering that Queen Catherine was such a supporter of the New Faith. He suspected she might be a secret Protestant.

"Don't be seen sharing your opinions too often. We must conform to the King's wishes," he said.

But he needn't have warned her. She had seen how quick the King was to act when he felt he wasn't being obeyed. Thomas Moore had tried to stand up to him, and look what happened to him. A head on a spike was his reward for years of service. Thomas Cromwell tried to push too much for reform and forced an ill-suited wife on the King. He suffered the same fate.

The King was the Head of the Church, and, though it may have been wrong to close monasteries and confiscate the lands of the Church, Frances was not about to argue with her uncle.

She had no wish to be martyred.

The tricky part was keeping up with the King's ever-changing mind and moods. But she looked to her father — the only one to survive so long in the King's good graces — and she had managed to follow from his example.

Frances looked at the straight back of Catherine Parr and wondered how long it would be before her uncle tired of her. She would say a special prayer every day that she was able to survive.

The day was not filled with lectures, though, and the Queen had hired a group of venetian minstrels. After the lecture was done, she called for them and they enjoyed music until it was time for supper.

∽

"You look well in crimson," Frances said, adjusting the Queen's hood.

The red velvet gown was cut in the Italian fashion, and, coupled with the French hood, Catherine looked stunning, but she was frowning and looked uncomfortable.

"What is wrong?"

"A woman should *wear such apparel as becommeth holiness and comely usage, with soberness.*"

Frances laughed. "You are a Queen. How can you be comely?"

"I do not wish to appear... extravagant."

"There is no reason for you to worry. You are expected some level of extravagance. The King would be most displeased if you stick to your dowdy gowns. Don't think the other ladies and I haven't noticed that you ordered nothing but dull colored fabrics."

For the first time, it was clear to Frances that Catherine had not been bred for such a high office. She had not been raised at court and had not seen how things were done. It might have been commendable for her to dress conservatively in the country, but, here at court, there were different expectations — no matter what the priests preached.

"I shall order something more suitable," Catherine said.

"That is good, your grace," Frances replied, finding it funny to show such deference to her though she had seen those even lower than Catherine rise to power and positions that should have been beyond them. "May I also suggest a Dutch jeweler — Mister Richardson."

"I have heard of him. I shall write to him."

"You should have your secretary do so," Frances reminded her gently.

If it wasn't for Catherine's sweetness, then Frances would be tempted to think ill of the new Queen, but it had been only mere weeks since her marriage to the King and she was still growing used to her position.

"As we are alone for the moment, might I ask you a favor?" Frances said.

"If I can, I will see it done."

"I believe my daughter Jane would flourish at court among your ladies. She is young but very learned. She does nothing but study..."

"You can stop," she interrupted. "I would love to have her at court."

"Very well, I shall speak to my husband. She can join the court at Christmas." Frances was exuberant. She knew she was grinning from ear to ear. Catherine mistook her excitement.

"I have it within my power to give those closest to me positions at court. I am more than happy to give you this. Though, if I could ask anything of you in return, it would be that you reconcile with the Duchess of Suffolk."

Frances took a sharp intake of breath; she tried to hide

the flash of fury that crossed her face at the mere mention of that woman.

"I... cannot, but I have been respectful, have I not?"

Now it was Catherine's turn to laugh. She didn't say anything else on the matter as her sister the Countess Hertford came in holding a box of jewels.

~

Jane at Bradgate was pensive when she was told that she would be joining Catherine's court. It was another distinct difference between Frances and her daughter. She had leapt at the chance to go to court, but Jane seemed to think of it as a trial for her to bear.

"What is the matter with you, Jane?" Frances was irked.

"I wish to stay here and study."

"This isn't about what you wish to do. You are to serve your family as the bible says you are to obey your mother and father." Frances felt ridiculous quoting the bible to her young child, but it was the only effective way to get her to listen.

"And what does father say?"

"He thinks it is a very good idea."

Frances was not exaggerating. He was surprised by the news but ecstatic to have his daughter shown off at court where everyone could see her brilliance.

"Then I shall do as you wish," she said.

Frances rolled her eyes at the solemnness with which she spoke and searched within her for some shred of patience.

"The Queen enjoys studying and she is planning to

learn Latin, Greek and even Hebrew. You shall find many of the ladies of her court are intellectually inclined. You shall have the very best tutors around you. I promise you shall enjoy it. Before you know it, we will be home."

This finally seemed to spark an interest in the young girl.

"But there shall be dancing. I shall be expected to dance."

"You are a lovely dancer," Frances said, thinking she was worried about her skill as she had been at her age.

Jane scrunched up her nose. "But it is not good to be seen to dance. A good Christian woman does not parade around..."

"Am I to be lectured to by my own child?" Frances threw up her arms. "I am going riding. This is ridiculous."

She left Jane in the library and walked to the stable yard. Her master of horse came running up beside her.

"My lady, what can I help you with? They told me you wished to go riding."

"Yes," she threw over her shoulder. "I was just planning to go for a bit. Not an actual hunting party."

"It would be wise to take someone with you," he said.

"Master Stokes, I believe I have nothing to fear in my own lands."

He looked as though he was about to argue but could do nothing more than bow. She watched him call for the groom to bring out her horse. He ran a hand over the horse's haunches and checked to ensure the shoes were on properly. He grinned almost shyly at her when he noticed her watching.

"Force of habit," he said. "The blacksmith had them on badly before."

"I'm glad to see you take so much care of my safety and those of my family."

Once she was in the saddle, she rode away without looking back.

~

The court had moved around a lot during her absence. The plague was spreading throughout the town and everyone was trying to find some safe refuge.

Finally, her husband returned home. Frances welcomed him back with a feast of stewed lamb and pottage followed by other rich dishes.

"Queen Catherine has her talons in the King," he said as he stretched before climbing into bed after her.

"How so?"

"He does her every bidding. She is often by his side, tending to him during one of his episodes."

"I do not envy her that." Frances thought of her uncle's wounds and many ailments. "Besides, this is the way he always is at the beginning. And it is better for us that he listens to her and not to some other advisor. You should be happy she is for the reform, is she not?"

"I am. I am," he repeated.

Frances knew immediately he was lying. "He is so fickle there is no point trying to earn his ear now."

He kissed her forehead. "I know."

She did not let him see her roll her eyes. She knew him

well enough by now that he imagined if he had his chance then he would be able to become the King's advisor as Cromwell and Wolsey had done before him. But he was not an astute politician or lawyer. He had dreams of grandeur, but he could not see them through himself. Besides, the risk was too great.

It was better to bide their time and wait for the perfect opportunity.

~

"Jane is an angel. You must be so proud," Queen Catherine congratulated her.

"I am," she responded, though there was no heart behind it. "I often find myself worrying that she is much too serious for a girl."

"Nonsense, you must foster this devotion to study and God in her. There are worse things for a girl to be."

"That is true." She thought of that flirt Katherine Howard with disgust.

"Are you sure you shall return to Bradgate after the holidays?"

"Yes, I enjoy overseeing my lands and the country air agrees with me." In truth, she did not mind avoiding court while Katherine Willoughby was still residing there.

"Very well." Queen Catherine seemed to know what she was thinking.

After mass, she met with her father in his rooms. His tall frame seemed to be hunched over, and he was looking more and more like a sickly old man than the strong soldier he had been in her youth.

"Father." She curtseyed to him.

"It has felt like a long time since I have spoken to you," he said idly.

"How are you?" she asked, seeking to avoid bringing up any unsavory topics.

"I am well. Sometimes I am sick with ague, but the doctors provide me with their potions and I am better for a time."

"You should be resting."

Her father laughed. "I am not an old man yet. There is still so much to do."

"I am sorry, I did not mean to insult you." She shifted from one foot to another. "I want what's best for you."

"You are a sweet girl to worry for your father so, but it also shows me how far I have fallen that my daughter dotes on me." He sighed heavily.

"As you know, the King is intent on war with France again. I shall go to command his armies. Before we leave I shall write my will..."

"Father!"

"...but I wish for things between us to be settled. I know there have been difficulties since your beloved mother passed away," he continued ignoring her protests.

Under her father's gaze, Frances felt like a girl again, freshly married and hurt by his choice to remarry.

"I cannot command your obedience any more, but I would hope that you could bring yourself to forgive me."

She was silent for a long moment. Of course, there was no way she could deny his request. He put her in an impossible position. The more she looked at him, the more pity she felt for him. He too had lost his wife. He had lived a long and hard life despite the favor of the King.

"Of course, I forgive you father," she said with as much sincerity as she could muster.

"You must understand I acted for the benefit of this family," he went on. "I loved your mother very much and I think of her often."

Frances wasn't sure if this was the sweet-talking courtier speaking to her or her father speaking from his heart. There was no way for her to tell and she felt a twinge of distrust.

Seeing she was tongue-tied her father smiled. "I am very happy to see you so well settled. Your mother would be proud."

She nearly flinched at his heavy hand placed on her shoulder. He must know her very little if he thought she was happily settled. And she thought with a wry smile, he knew little of her relationship with her mother. She would not have been proud. She had never been proud of her.

Her life had been nothing but constant strife and filled with unhappiness. Just recently, she suffered the death of two children and the supplanting of her husband's affections.

But her father saw her smile and misunderstood. "I hope we shall have more time to spend together. That husband of yours does well for himself in Parliament."

"Thank you, I do as well. I hope you shall rally your strength."

She escaped his rooms as quickly as she could.

CHAPTER SIX

1544-1546

FRANCES STOOD on the dockside watching the ships departing. Beside her, the ladies of the court were cheering, ahead of her was the Queen. Just as Catherine Parr was standing erect and magisterial so was Frances.

For many, the thought of war brought images of glory and fortune, but Frances was not a fool to think that the people closest to her were invincible. All it would take would be a stray arrow or misfired canon shot and her husband would perish. She also knew that diseases common on the battlefield could just as easily end his life.

Looking at the Queen Regent, she was sure Catherine felt the same. King Henry had been unwell, the doctors had advised that he did not lead the army himself. Now it seemed like he was setting out to prove something.

Her father, too, was on board, serving as a commander

in the English army. These men should be at home being cared for in their old age, but, instead, they were risking their lives and those of many others to prove to the world they were still strong. They dreamed of reliving their glory days and marching into Paris, but Frances was not so naïve.

She had begged Henry to stay behind with her. The Queen would need advisors at her side to help her with the rule of the Kingdom, but he would not hear of it. So she would have to rely on the power of prayer that he would return home to her safe and sound.

The Queen returned to London, and Frances accompanied her in her train.

She was surprised by the change she found in her friend who was once so hesitant on the throne. The love lavished on her by the King and her own tenacity now shined forth. Gone was the meek Queen. In her place was the woman who was writing admonishing letters to the Universities.

Frances had to struggle to keep from laughing as Catherine seemed unable to hold in her passion.

"You cannot lecture preachers."

"How can I remain silent when they are so obviously wrong?" Catherine all but raged.

"There is nothing wrong with a little discourse." Lady Anne Herbert took her side.

Seeing herself outnumbered Frances shrugged.

"It just seems dangerous to stray into areas out of our understanding."

"Do you really believe that women cannot study and understand the word of God as well as men?" Catherine looked horrified.

Frances knew that this was indeed what she had been

taught, but she thought of her little Jane at home with her nose in her books and shook her head.

"No, but I do think they do not like us debating and arguing with them." She smiled to lighten the mood. "But I shall leave you to your writing. I was told I have a horse to see in the stables."

"There's more to life than riding," Catherine called after her as she left.

"Hardly, your grace," Frances said with a curtsey.

Within a few days Frances was pining for home, but she felt as though she couldn't leave just yet.

It was at court that she could hear the news of the English army firsthand. She didn't want to wait for it to trickle down to her or to wait for Henry's unreliable letters.

"I shall send for Elizabeth to join us. I don't believe she is thriving at Ashridge. She is of a nervous disposition and I know being housed in that dissolved religious college must be uncomfortable," Catherine mused, as if she was trying to debate with herself.

Frances couldn't help but agree, there would be nothing comfortable in those cold stone halls. Definitely nothing for a young girl to amuse herself.

"You shall do as you wish," she remarked.

"I don't believe the King would object." Catherine made an off-hand remark. "I wish she was allowed to spend more time at court."

"You are regent. You can gather whatever lords and ladies you want around yourself," Frances encouraged her.

She did not comment that the King did not like seeing his daughter for she reminded him of her mother. She did not need to remind Catherine of the many wives that came before her.

Elizabeth was definitely pleased to be summoned to court. She received many gifts from her doting step-mother. Frances wondered if Catherine wasn't doting on her too much. But no one could accuse Catherine of being a bleeding heart. She was ruthless when she wanted to be.

Frances saw this firsthand when the Earl of Shrewsbury asked for an audience with her.

"I have proof that the Earl of Cumberland was hunting illegally on my lands, your grace. I have written to him but he refuses to stop and says I am mistaken. Twice my steward has caught him."

Queen Catherine, sitting on her throne under the cloth of estate, tutted under her breath.

"There can be no petty squabbles amongst ourselves while we are at war."

"Of course not. I wished to draw this to your attention so that you may speak to him if you are able to." The Earl was apologetic. "It is not right that while the King is away all law is ignored."

"No, it is not right. I shall write to the Earl of Cumberland myself." Her sharp tone indicated that she would show him no patience. "I promise you that he shall compensate you for your loss."

"Thank you, milady." He bowed deeply to her, then, without turning his back on her, walked out of the presence chamber.

"That was very well put," Katherine Willoughby spoke. "How can the nobles be squabbling at a time like this?"

Frances saw her wring a kerchief in her hands. She had looked jumpy and hard pressed ever since her husband had left for France. Frances felt a twinge of pity for her. She knew how it was to worry over a husband gone off to war. Even more so that she knew how her father's health was failing faster than ever.

She shook her head, trying to clear the thoughts from her mind. There was no point worrying over nothing.

~

The guns of London Tower sounded to announce the King's triumphant victory and return. The English army had not marched on Paris but rather laid siege to Boulogne. The city finally surrendered.

There was much celebrating in the streets at the news.

Frances's own father was presented the keys to the city by the mayor. Her husband had been there as well, a proud captain. He had returned to her, though the English army was still in France. She was surprised to find he wasn't playing the part of the triumphant soldier upon his return. He did not wish to discuss it with her at all.

"It was not all games and chivalry, you know," he snapped when she had pressed him harder.

"I never said..."

He looked at her apologetically, and pulled her into his arms squeezing her tightly.

"I apologize. I should not trouble my wife with such matters. But the campaign was hard and hard won. It is hardly worth it if we cannot press forward and capture more lands," he whispered into her hair. "But I don't want to discuss it."

"Alright," she agreed.

The court celebrated the victory for days, though, and it was hard to escape talks of battles. Those who had not gone to France were eager to go themselves, while those who had been there were tight-lipped.

It soon trickled down that the English army had suffered great losses for their victory. Her father was still stationed there, but they were running out of supplies and the men were threatening to desert from lack of pay or hunger.

When news that the English army had retreated back to Calais there was hell to pay. The King was furious.

Scared of the King's reaction, Frances ran to the Queen's rooms. If anyone might temper his reaction, it was Catherine.

"My father would never betray the King," Frances said quickly to Catherine, who was listening intently. "The King must understand that my father had no choice but to act as he did."

Catherine took her hands in hers. "Don't fret, I shall speak to him. I am sure his councilors will help him see reason."

Frances couldn't stop the shiver that ran down her back.

"They may turn against him too. They are angry about the cost of the war and ready to blame someone. They scent blood in the water."

"The Duchess of Suffolk also spoke to me."

Frances could see Catherine was trying hard to reassure her, but the fear building in her chest would not subside.

"You have no reason to fear for your father. The King shall be reassured and will rally. He heard rumors that your father was unwell and was very concerned."

Frances bit her lip.

"Why don't you speak to Katherine Willoughby? The two of you may comfort each other."

Frances pulled away. "I cannot. But thank you for your help and kind words."

She left the Queen's rooms to go find Henry. He would understand.

∼

She was wearing black again, walking through the halls of Norwich Place with a heavy heart. She had rarely visited her father's London residence and now this might be the last time she did so.

Her father had died quietly in the night. A messenger had appeared at her door first thing in the morning. She was sure only the King heard the news before her.

She entered his bedroom to find him washed and dressed in his robes of estate. Against his pillows, he looked almost as though he was sleeping peacefully. It was Katherine, covered by a black veil and visibly sobbing by his bedside, that spoiled the illusion.

Finally, being here made her hesitate. Being faced with death once again, she couldn't help but tremble. There was new life growing in her womb, and she wondered if it would be tainted by being so close to death. A hand crept over the small bulge in fear.

"Frances, he is gone," Katherine said between sobs.

"May he find peace in Heaven." She took a seat opposite of Katherine, avoiding looking at the pallid face of her father and, instead, focused on the ermine fur trimming the edge of his robe. "Queen Catherine sent me a message that the King is quite devastated. He will come pay his respects as well, before they take his body away."

"How can you be so cold?"

Frances was taken aback by the accusation. "I-I lost my father today. It is hard for me to accept."

Katherine was back to sobbing. "I'm sorry. I know. I am only thinking of myself."

Frances wished to leave, but seeing the honest grief displayed by Katherine made her stay. She hadn't thought that Katherine would be broken up about Charles's death. She thought of her young sons and knew that their wardship would pass to the crown. Katherine might be separated from her sons.

Her heart was struck by sudden pity for her friend. Katherine must have thought the worst was over when she had seen him return from war and survive the King's displeasure. But he had worked himself to the bone for the King's service, and it had worn away his remaining health. At least he left behind two male heirs to continue the family name.

Frances thought of the child in her belly and said a prayer that this too was a son. She would name him Charles for her father.

"He wishes to be buried quietly at Tattershall," Katherine said in-between another bout of crying.

Frances was unsure of what to say and merely nodded. The King would not hear of such a simple funeral for his greatest friend. He paid to have his funeral at St. George's chapel.

Even in death her father was obedient to the King.

∼

There was a change in the air. With the new year, the King's mood seemed to shift. He was regressing back to his conservative views. This was evident by his favoring Gardiner and his cronies.

Frances returned from hawking, handing her falcon back to Adrian Stokes.

"See that she is well fed," Frances said, petting the bird's cream colored chest. She had been one of her first gifts from Henry, and she had grown into an excellent hunter. Despite her age, she was flying well and Frances wouldn't be parted from her just yet.

She returned to the Queen's rooms to find a lively discussion happening on the meaning of scripture. The Queen had become quite the scholar and even published anonymously Psalms and Prayers in English with the support of Cranmer. It was an open secret that she was continuing such work.

It was unheard of, but, at the time, the King was encouraging. Now Frances worried what he might think of this.

Katherine Willoughby, the widow of her father, had returned to court. It seemed her tears had dried up, and she was happy to take center stage. The King seemed to pay special attention to her ever since her return. He gave her little gifts and invited her to play cards with him.

Frances was suspicious of this and wondered if Queen Catherine could see the signs.

The Spanish ambassador found his way to her at dinner. He liked to pay attention to her ever since the King had signed his will and declared the act of succession.

"My lady, I wonder if you have heard the troubling news?"

Frances was too much of a courtier to gape at him like a puppy desperate for a treat.

"Nothing to trouble me," she said.

"Ah, perhaps not but you may not have heard the King is interested in taking another wife."

Frances did not even blink, though her heart was beating faster in her chest. "Who might that be?"

"The dowager Duchess of Suffolk seems to be the candidate."

"It's all rumor, of course. The King loves the Queen and showers her with affection and trust."

"As you say." He tilted his head in agreement.

She spent some more time talking to him, though she wished to run to Queen's rooms to warn her. At the same time, anger flared in her gut at the thought of Katherine having such shameful ambitions.

Frances could not support such a thing. It was disgusting.

It was Katherine who she descended upon first, finding her walking down the halls alone.

"I thought you loved my father, but I see you would

disrespect him by chasing after a married man. I thought Queen Catherine was your friend. Then again, you hardly care about your 'friends' at all, do you?" she spat as venomously as she could.

Katherine looked taken aback, but she too narrowed her eyes. "I don't know what you are talking about."

"You are chasing after a second husband and will push the Queen aside to get what you want. You've always been such a flirt, proud of your looks."

"You are projecting your own insecurities on me." She tilted her head almost as though she was sorry for her.

Frances couldn't bear it.

"You will leave court!"

"You cannot command me. You have no idea what I struggle with. The King could take away his favor any moment. I am living on an edge, one misstep and I might lose everything, my sons, my lands. Everything."

The two of them squared off at each other, neither backing down.

"You seem awfully content pawing at an older married man. Don't think that the whole court doesn't know what a shameless whore you have been."

"I need not stay to hear this. I am sorry I was not born into the position you have been. I shall pray you never have to fight for your supper and worry that everything you hold can be taken away on someone's whim."

Frances watched, stunned, as Katherine strode away. The swishing of her gown the only sound in the corridor. She wished she hadn't let her anger get the better of her. She had no proof that Katherine was seeking to seduce her uncle, the King.

Still she did not stop in her quest to warn the Queen. Rumors always had some grain of truth in them. If the Queen had displeased the King in some way, then she needed to be warned.

"Katherine is innocent," the Queen protested. "Or at the very least she does not do what hundreds of other girls do. But I am married to the King, and he can have no complaints or grounds against me. I have served him well."

Frances shook her head. "It's not her you should be worried about but your husband. It doesn't matter how perfect you have been, he will find a reason to put you aside. The truth doesn't matter. Gardiner is his lapdog again and you know how conservative he is. He sees you as an obstacle. You read forbidden books, and you study..."

"There is nothing wrong with study," Catherine threw back at her. "The King himself has encouraged it."

"The King can change his mind." Frances wondered why she bothered. As her frustration grew, she found herself longing for some wine.

"I'll speak to my sister to see what more she can find out. I find this all so laughable. We haven't been married long and we are still happy."

Frances did not point out that many of his wives did not last long, but she did her duty by her.

That night she told Henry she was returning to Bradgate.

"I shall send you home with a doctor to see Mary," he said.

It put her on edge. Her last pregnancy had resulted in another daughter and not the son they had wished for. More than that, she suspected her daughter was a dwarf.

She was incredibly small for her age, though her husband was adamant that nothing was wrong. She had suggested they send Mary away to be raised elsewhere, but he wouldn't hear of it.

They had a row for the first time in months over the subject.

"I will send Jane to you then. It would be good for her to visit court."

"Very well."

On her way to her favorite house, she stopped by to see Mary at Hunsdon. As if sensing her father's growing dislike of the Queen, she too had retreated away from court for a respite.

They walked together arm in arm through the gardens, enjoying the fresh air.

"The Queen is very good to me. She sends me clothes and presents and always gives me a place at court," Mary said, but Frances could hear the 'but' left unsaid and looked at her pressing her for more information.

"I worry she has been led astray into heresy," Mary admitted.

Frances nodded. She didn't say anything on the matter. Mary would call her husband a heretic too. She remained resolute to follow the King's wishes and worship as her husband did.

"I shall pray no harm comes to her," Mary continued. "She is a good woman."

"And friend," Frances added.

～

Frances was overseeing the construction of a new bear pit when she spotted a retinue of horses riding up to the house. She left the workers and went towards the courtyard to see who it was. She was surprised to find Jane riding pillion behind her husband's secretary. An armed guard accompanying them along with Jane's nurse.

"What is it? What happened?" She had received no news of her arrival, and she could sense the tension in the courtyard.

"The Earl commanded me to ride to Bradgate with the young lady." The man doffed his cap to her.

Another helped Jane down from the saddle, and Frances rounded on her.

"Did your father say anything?"

Jane handed her a letter but whispered. "The Queen's ladies were taken in for questioning."

Frances did a double take. So the rumors were true.

"Everyone was leaving court if they could," Jane said, her eyes now teary.

"And the Duchess of Suffolk?"

"She left too."

Frances found herself breathing a sigh of relief that she wasn't at court lording over everyone. But this did not mean much. The King always sent his favorites away while he was "divorcing" his unwanted wives.

In her solar, she dismissed her ladies and read Henry's letter in private.

It turned out Gardiner had emerged publicly as an enemy of the Queen. He had arrested and tortured Anne Askew, though she had confessed to nothing. But he was not after low-born heretics. He wished to take down the Queen.

She sat down at her desk and penned a careful letter, knowing that it might be opened and searched by Gardiner's men. She urged her husband to come home. He was known too widely to be a supporter of the reformed faith. With Gardiner hunting down reformers, he might be next.

She thought of the wily Catherine Parr and knew in her heart that she would find a way to survive.

CHAPTER SEVEN

1547-1551

THE BELLS WERE PEELING BACKWARDS. Frances was in a rush to get back to London where her husband was waiting for her. She did not worry about gowns, knowing that she could draw mourning clothes from the royal wardrobe but worried about the roads in February.

By the time she got to London, it was nearly time for her uncle to be entombed. Henry helped her down from her horse, dressed in black and wearing a sour expression.

"What is it, husband?" she asked kissing him on the mouth.

"Gardiner is saying the mass even though the King died holding Cranmer's hand." He shook his head disapprovingly. "He wants a mass said for his soul in the old papist way."

"He was always fickle." Frances shrugged. "And the

council? Prin—King Edward is still so young? Has the King's will been read?"

Her husband turned a scornful look to her as though she was as naïve as their daughters.

"Yes, for they kept the King's death secret for days while they consolidated power. I wasn't invited to this inner circle. Edward Seymour has been named Lord Protector. In effect, he shall rule for his nephew. They say they shall make him a Duke."

Frances nearly growled. "He doesn't deserve such an honor. You should be made a Duke."

Her husband looked almost defeated. "I shall focus on my studies. They shall come to see they need me. I don't need to go begging Seymour for favor."

"No, of course not. You shouldn't debase yourself like that."

The funeral procession left Westminster and hundreds of mourners followed the King's coffin and effigy. The larger than life monarch was laid to rest in as grand a manner as he had been in life. They stopped at Syon House for the night — showing once again the power of the Lord Protector.

The next day, Frances was with the Queen in the Queen's closet where they watched Henry being interned with Jane Seymour. For years he had still favored her above all other wives, and Frances knew firsthand how it grated on Catherine to have a dead woman take precedence over her.

She wondered what Catherine thought seeing Henry honor his favorite wife in this way. But Catherine's eyes were dry, and she seemed lighthearted. In essence, she had been set free.

After Gardiner's attack on her, she had been subdued;

she worried over everything she said and stopped hearing lectures that weren't expressly approved by the King.

Now she could do as she wished.

Frances did not miss the way her eyes moved away from the coffin to the Seymour brothers. The younger, Thomas, seemed just as distracted. His handsome dark head tilted up towards the private chapel as if sensing her stare though he could not see her.

Frances couldn't help but wonder.

～

They stayed on in London until February not wishing to miss the coronation of her cousin. It was imperative they be seen at court. After all, Frances was in line for the throne.

She would never say it out loud, but with Prince Edward being so young and his sisters still being considered formally illegitimate, she had begun to dream of the crown of England sitting on her own head. She had always dreamed of such a position for herself.

When she was younger she dreamed of marrying a Prince or a King. Now she dreamed of ruling herself.

But she dared not think on this for long, fearing that somehow someone would peer into her soul and see her treasonous desires. Nor did she confess these thoughts to her confessor. There was no safety for her there. So she took her sinful thoughts and begged God for forgiveness every night.

Thankfully, like his father, Prince Edward was fair and well-built. Dressed in white velvet and a sable coat, he looked magnificent for a nine-year-old boy. It was hard to imagine that this boy was the head of the English Church.

Her husband was the King's sword bearer, a role he had played often for King Henry. It was perhaps not the illustrious role he would have hoped for, but he was happy enough to be placed apart from the other nobility.

A dais had been erected in Westminster. The Abbey was transformed from the dark blacks and blues of a funeral to gold and silver. A throne was placed center stage. Frances noted the cushions placed upon it to make the young Prince look taller.

Archbishop Cranmer performed the ceremony and anointed Edward as King of England. Holding the orb and scepter, with a crown on his head, King Edward waited as the nobility approached and swore fealty to him, kissing his left cheek.

There was feasting in the great hall after, in the usual extravagant fashion. More celebrations were to follow at Whitehall.

Frances curtseyed low to the boy King and kissed his cheek.

"Your Majesty, I was honored to witness your coronation ceremony," she said. "I know how proud your blessed father and mother would have been to see you on this day."

"Thank you, cousin Frances."

He may have only been nine, but he spoke with the self-importance of someone much older.

"Your husband has served me well," he continued.

"Thank you. I know we all endeavor to serve you." She curtseyed again as he nodded and walked backwards away from the dais.

Henry was riled from what he saw as further insults to himself.

"John Dudley, Thomas Seymour, William Parr... they all have new titles and have been elevated above their rank. If I have served him so well, where is my title?"

Frances hushed him and took the cup of wine in his hands.

"I think, perhaps, we should retire for the night," she suggested calmly. There was no need for the whole court to know of his animosity. This was no time to make enemies.

∾

They received a strange visitor at Bradgate one day in early March. He had ridden up to their great house unannounced with a small retinue of attendants. Frances was surprised to be receiving Thomas Seymour, who had never been a great friend of theirs, into her home, but she did her best to be a good host.

Henry seemed just as apprehensive as her.

"Lord Seymour, what can we do for you?" her husband asked, not beating around the bush.

Thomas smiled at his frankness. Frances imagined a grinning snake and was on alert.

"I have come to inquire about your daughter, the Lady Jane."

"What about her?" Frances asked, apprehensive. She looked at Thomas and wondered if he had any designs on her daughter, but she was too young to be a prospective bride for him.

"She has always been friendly with King Edward since their youth."

Frances wondered if they were still not children.

"And she is of an age that she could be placed in a household to further her education."

"We provide her the very best tutors here," Frances scowled.

Thomas turned to her. The smile faltering on his lips.

"I meant no offence. But I believe she would do very well in the household of the Dowager Queen Catherine or my own at Seymour Place in London."

"I don't understand why you would trouble yourself over this matter?" Henry spoke up. "What interest is it of yours?"

Frances was quicker on the uptake and she peered at Thomas suspiciously. Had he dared to strike up a relationship with the Dowager Queen so soon after the death of the King? There could be no other explanation.

"I have it in my power to place Lady Jane in the Dowager Queen's company. It is my design to see her married to King Edward."

Frances's glass smashed on the ground as it fell out of her hand in shock. Silence descended upon the room. Henry dismissed his gentleman usher from the room.

"How... why would King Edward marry my daughter?" he asked.

Frances could see the sheen of greed in his eye as he imagined his daughter being crowned Queen.

"He knows her and has always been fond of her. Her position is such that it would be an advantageous marriage, seeing as she has royal Tudor blood, from her mother." He nodded in Frances direction.

"He would marry a Princess. Why should he marry an English girl?" Frances frowned, not believing Seymour for a second.

"His father did before him," Thomas said, with a casual shrug as if this was a small matter to overcome.

"That is not enough assurance to be plotting with you."

"Frances," Henry said with a tone that told her to stop.

"This is no plot." Thomas turned on the charm again. "Merely an agreement between two old families."

Frances wanted to say that the Seymours had only risen to greatness through their sister, but she kept silent.

"King Edward is my nephew, I am his favorite uncle." He ignored Frances's snort of disbelief. "It would be a simple matter to convince him. I would, of course, pay for the wardship of Lady Jane so that I might bring about this settlement that would be beneficial for both of us."

Frances could see Henry was sorely tempted by this. She was thinking of herself though when she interrupted.

"You must give us time so we can dwell on this matter. It cannot be decided so quickly. I am sure you understand. We love our daughter very much."

If he was annoyed he did not show it. "Of course, I know how you care for your children very much."

Frances did not even bother to be insulted by the back-handed compliment. She rose out of her chair and encouraged her husband to do the same.

"I shall make sure you have the very best rooms and anything you could wish."

Seymour went back to London the following morning,

but Frances knew that was not the last she would see of him. In another day, John Harington, Thomas Seymour's trusted servant, appeared on their doorstep.

It took three days, but the man managed to wear down her husband and she could hardly protest. Even if the plan were not to succeed, they would still gain two thousand pounds for his effort. Money was needed to settle their debts and Jane would be placed in the household of a great lady of the realm. What was the problem?

There was hardly anything she could argue against. Except in her heart she felt set aside once again. If they plotted to put Jane on the throne, then that would mean she would never get to sit there herself.

Another part of her knew this would be a most advantageous marriage she could make for her daughter. It would raise her and their whole family to the pinnacle of power in the Kingdom. Perhaps they could surpass the Seymour family.

With an initial payment of five hundred pounds paid in coin, Frances oversaw her daughter sent off to Seymour Place. She went without complaint, though seeing her now-pretty daughter ride off left Frances feeling a twinge of worry in her heart.

They had been reassured Jane would be looked after by several women of good breeding. Harington had also suggested and hinted that the Dowager Queen had remarried or would do so soon to his master, for they were very much in love.

Frances did not need him to spell it out for her but found safety in playing dumb.

What would King Edward think of this? She doubted

the country would react positively to hasty secret marriage. But if anyone was clever enough to come out of this mess on top it was Thomas Seymour. But one thing was certain; the secret that Catherine Parr had married Thomas Seymour would not remain so for long.

Mary Tudor was livid at the news that her stepmother had insulted her father's memory with such a marriage. Frances was there as she railed against the woman who had been so kind to her.

"I shall never speak to her again," she swore.

Frances wanted to calm her but let her finish ranting.

"I hear that the Lord Protector is upset by the marriage, but the King has forgiven them and allowed the marriage."

"Did you know he has written to me privately to stop hearing Mass? As if he could command me!" Mary turned her rage away from Catherine.

"Your brother... was educated in the reformed faith. He likely wishes to continue the work of your father," Frances speculated.

She did not point out that her daughters were being raised in the same fashion. Perhaps Mary thought of her as a Catholic still, but she could hardly turn her back on her husband's religion.

"I pray that when he comes into his majority, he will realize his error. I pray God will help him see the light. But for now, bad advisors cloud his judgement," Mary said, stalking the rooms.

"Troubling times indeed," Frances mused.

"What?" Mary had not heard her.

"I am sorry for the troubles between your brother and yourself."

This was not the end but the beginning of a drama that played out far from Bradgate. As she watched the bear baiting in the pit, and rode through her large parkland, the councilors were grumbling. Many thought Seymour should be arrested and that Catherine had lost all right on the dower lands left to her by the King.

Frances swore she would visit Catherine at Chelsea Manor soon but found a peace in the tranquility of neutral ground. She did not wish to get involved in such squabbles. At least Jane had Catherine to look after her now. She could sleep easier knowing that.

～

Shaking with fear, Frances ran down the steps of Bradgate. The red brick house was not meant to be a defensible castle. There was no moat or cannons that could be shot from the turrets. They had only a small retinue of yeomen.

The rest of the household could be issued weapons but they were hardly soldiers, and, if those attacking were their family members, then they could hardly be trusted to stay loyal.

Even from here she could hear the bells of the church tolling. All Frances knew was that a gang of armed papists had gathered in the town nearby. It was reminiscent of the previous year when reformists stormed into the churches, pulling down rood screens and smashing windows. They had felt no fear then, believing that the Lord Protector would send an army to quell the rebellions and make an example of the traitors.

He had failed to do so.

Now the people felt safe to rise again. She didn't know what was happening, but they weren't safe here if they decided to take their revenge upon the gentry for trying to impose the English prayer book.

She cursed Henry for being in London at such a time.

There was no time to pack away their items. A gown and night shift were thrown haphazardly in a cloth sack. Her jewels were locked up and she retrieved a heavy purse of gold from their coffers.

"Girls, are you ready?" She was in the stable yard, a flurry of activity all around her as the servants and attendants rushed to prepare for them to leave.

Jane, talking to John Aylmer, looked at her and nodded.

"Get on your horse then. There will be time for lessons later." Frances turned to her younger two daughters. They were riding pillion behind two trust yeomen.

Adrian Stokes had the reins of her horse in his hand. She accepted his help into the saddle.

"You are to ride with us?" She hadn't meant for it to sound like a question.

"My lord would never forgive me if I let you go unattended. I have some military experience if it comes to that." He touched a hand to the dagger at his belt.

They would ride hard for the safety of London. Their small party should be able to pass unmolested.

"No banners," Frances shouted, seeing some silly servant bring one out. "We don't want to announce to the world who we are."

By noon, they set off at a break neck speed. As soon as they put Leicester behind them, they slowed their pace. Though anyone could see the tension on the face of their company.

They stopped at Apethorpe Palace for the night. The staff was surprised to find them at their gates, but, upon realizing who Frances was, they opened the gates and made rooms ready.

This was one of Lady Elizabeth's homes in Northampton. Frances would not have wished to stay in her home after all the business with Thomas Seymour, but there was hardly time to be picky and safe lodgings were hard to come by.

Jane might have felt uncomfortable as well, but she didn't let her thoughts be known. She had seen firsthand Elizabeth's flirtations with Seymour and the devastation it caused to Catherine Parr.

Frances said a silent prayer for the soul of her departed friend. She had given Seymour a child but paid the ultimate price. She thought sadly of how excited Catherine had been when she wrote to Frances the news that she was with child.

Ever since her marriage to him, she had faced difficulties on all fronts.

The council disapproved, the Lord Protector refused to give her the royal jewels left to her by King Henry, her family and the public at large muttered about her behavior. The popularity she had gained as Queen of England seemed to vanish in one stroke.

Though she had continued to study and publish, she must have felt besieged. So the news that she would become a mother must have lifted her spirits.

Frances kept a copy of Lamentations of a Sinner in her library, proud of her friend's achievements and in memory of her. She was glad Jane had not been dragged into the drama that followed the investigation into Thomas Seymour's behavior and intentions toward Elizabeth.

When news reached them that he was to be executed, Frances looked to her husband with a satisfied grin as if to say she knew he was trouble and would come to this.

Henry was at Dorset House and was pleased to see them arrive.

"Are you well?" he asked scanning his family.

"Tired but nothing a bit of rest won't help with, but you must tell me what madness is happening in the country."

"I shall." He patted her shaking hands. Turning to his girls, he commended them for their bravery and sent them inside.

In their private rooms, they dined on pheasant and meat pies while Frances listened to what he had to say.

"It is in Exeter that the worst of the trouble is happening. The papists have risen to rebel against the Act of Uniformity. They won't have an English prayer book in their churches. Those misguided fools," he shook his head.

"How serious is it?"

"They say there are over two thousand laying siege to Exeter."

Frances gasped.

"The council is pressuring Seymour to act."

Frances noted her husband's lack of respect for him. The rumors were true and Edward Seymour was losing his grip on power then.

"You shall stay here. London is the safest place for you now."

"I know that."

She didn't wish to be caught in the middle of a civil war.

～

Not even a week later, disastrous news reached London. Robert Kett, a landowner in Norfolk, had taken up leadership of a large army of over sixteen thousand who were rumored to be marching on Norwich.

Meanwhile, Lord Russel had refused to attack the rebels in Essex until the Lord Protector sent reinforcements. He seemed out of his wits and at a loss for what he should do. Frances did not envy him, but she had expected this to happen. An upstart like him with no royal blood in his veins could not command the country.

Henry came from court looking surprisingly jubilant.

"This is the start of his downfall," he promised her.

"It means nothing to us if someone else replaces him," Frances said.

He gave her a knowing smile, but, no matter how she pressured him, he would not reveal what he knew.

"We shall see how this plays out. Luck might turn and Seymour might take control again. There's no point giving you hope." Henry paused. "But I should tell you this. The Lord Protector has asked to speak to me of Jane. I think he wishes to arrange a marriage between his son and her.

"Tell me you didn't agree to it?"

"Nothing of the sort. I said I would think on it and perhaps an informal arrangement could be made." He was quick to add: "Nothing in writing. This way we have all sides covered, whether he retains power or not."

Frances nodded slowly. "He must be desperate for friends if he would agree to that."

"I believe he is."

~

Martial law was declared in London as news of Norwich falling to Kett and his men reached them. Frances did not leave Dorset House and ordered the girls to do the same. Jane was more than happy to comply.

She rolled her eyes at her daughter's piety. If she could, she would send her to a nunnery, for she belonged in quiet cloisters, not court. It irked her that with all the wealth of the family, she chose to dress plainly and wear as little jewelry as possible. It felt like a personal affront to herself, seeing as she liked dressing in bright colors and enjoyed wearing precious stones.

Her husband brought news of William Parr's defeat in Norwich, which was unsurprising given his lack of experience and being severely outnumbered. Meanwhile, in Essex, Lord Russel had laid waste to the rebellion. He hunted down men with a vengeance unexpected by the council.

Frances was sick to her stomach when she heard he had the throats of nine hundred men slit. Henry had maintained his good mood though, and she knew from this that something was afoot. Then one day he was no longer rowing down the river to Hampton Court but rather going to Westminster.

"Henry, are you sure this is wise?"

He kissed her brow, dismissing her concern with a wave of his hand.

"This is more than wise. We shall be on the winning side," he whispered in her ear.

She hated how dismissive he was of her and worried he had fallen for some other fool promising him the world.

~

By October the shocking news of Edward Seymour fleeing with the King to the defensible castle of Windsor was all over London. Seeing he was about to lose power, he had taken the drastic step of kidnapping his own nephew.

The newly formed council headed by none other than John Dudley, Earl of Warwick, chased after him. Frances thought Edward Seymour had gone very mad indeed.

Not even a week later he was being marched into the Tower.

Frances was invited to court, now a chief lady. Without having to watch Edward Seymour's wife parade around like a Queen, she enjoyed the luxuries it had to offer.

"I shall be given a seat on the Privy Council," Henry said.

But Frances was not interested, she was not surprised Henry was being given some reward for supporting Warwick. She only hoped he had not been bought cheaply.

"And the Lord Protector?"

"What about him?"

"What shall be done with him?"

Henry shrugged. "But he is lost for sure. He will never regain power."

Warwick proved to be more astute than Henry, however. The rebellions around the country were put down, and, though charges were laid on the Lord Protector, a sentence was not passed. He was popular with the common people and to sentence him now would be to spark more rebellions.

After Christmas of that year, he was released and even invited to sit on the Privy Council. Frances could smell a trap a mile away but had listened to her husband venting his frustration.

"It is embarrassing to see him every day. He knows me for a false friend. God help me if he ever has the power to bring me down."

"He won't."

But her reassurances went unheard.

The Earl of Warwick had shown himself to be a dangerous player. He had let Edward Seymour dig his own grave with his pride and ambition. Instead of accepting defeat, Edward had sought to take down John Dudley but was ill-prepared. Arrested on a felony charge, he was executed.

Frances watched the young King on his throne. He seemed untroubled by the recent death of his last uncle. Perhaps his upbringing had made him cold-hearted. A succession of mothers, and seeing his father's ruthlessness, had probably led him to being the same.

"I am happy to see you at court, Lady Frances."

Frances turned to find Jane Dudley standing before her. She gave the countess a respectful curtsey in greeting. She was still above her in rank, though her husband held the reins of the court in his hands.

"I am happy to be back."

"You must go hunting with me tomorrow."

"If the weather is good," she stipulated. She didn't like feeling as though Jane Dudley was being charitable towards her.

"Of course." The older woman managed a smile. "Shall your daughters join us?"

"Jane cannot be prevailed upon to leave her studies, I am afraid."

"Ah, that is unfortunate. Well, good evening."

Frances watched her weave her way around the crowds of courtiers, saying hello to her favorites. She asked Henry if there was any particular reason for the friendliness shown to her. She had become increasingly distrustful in her adult years.

"They need our support."

"It's as simple as that?"

"I wouldn't be surprised if they propose a marriage between our families. They don't have much noble blood in their veins, and Jane has not yet been betrothed."

"You know she thinks herself betrothed to that Seymour boy."

Henry waved away her fears. "She shall do as we please. We are her parents. But it is too soon to think of such things." He yawned. "I am going to retire."

She watched him go. He had not come to her bedroom for many a night nor invited her to share his. Did he think her an old woman past her prime already? She was only thirty-three.

Perhaps he thought there was no point, seeing as she had such a hard time getting with child.

She still hoped she could give him a son. Then their child might have an even better claim to the throne than the bastard Tudor Princesses. But if he had given up hope...

Thoughts of this riled her up. She knew she was handsome enough for a woman her age, and she certainly had the style and breeding of a desirable woman.

~

She shouldn't be smiling but she was. She would have to confess to this grievous sin later.

She took her letter directly to her husband, though he probably knew already. Her father's two sons and heirs had died of the sweat. The title and lands would pass to the King to dispose of as he wished, and Katherine Willoughby, had lost everything she had held.

A part of her understood the heavy loss Katherine had suffered and sympathized with her. The death of heirs was especially hard. On the other hand, now, as her father's next legal heir, she stood to benefit.

Henry did not look up from his papers as she walked into his office. She waited patiently for his attention, trying not to be irked. When he finally looked towards her she beamed at him.

"I have very sad news," she tempered, realizing being happy at the moment was ill advised. "My father's sons have died."

"Most unfortunate, I heard the Duke had taken ill, but I thought perhaps his brother had escaped."

"We shall attend the funeral, if there is time," Frances suggested.

"Yes, of course."

"And the title? Shall the King allow it to become extinct?"

Now she had her husband's full attention. He looked pensive as he played with the feathers of his quill.

"No, I suppose not. It would be such a waste."

"That's just what I thought." She smiled, walking around his desk and placing a kiss on his cheek. "You shall speak with John Dudley?"

He nodded. "The matter must be approached delicately."

"Of course," she said, happy they had come to some secret understanding. "Poor Katherine, though. She must be bereft."

He nodded.

She wondered if perhaps she could put aside her anger and reach out to her as a friend. No sooner had this thought crossed her mind than she felt her stubborn nature flare up, and she knew she couldn't bring herself to do it. It was too late to make amends.

Eventually, in an act of Christian charity and repentance of her sins, Frances wrote her a long letter. She expressed her sorrow for Katherine's loss of her sons — reminiscing that she knew the pain of this loss. She ended the letter asking for forgiveness for the harsh accusations she had made to Katherine following the death of her father.

$\sim$

Nothing, not even the chilly October wind, could ruin this day for Frances. She was dressed in her finest gown, dripping in jewels from head to toe. The ladies of the court now referred to her as Duchess, and she had received the ducal strawberry leaves she had always coveted as a child.

She wore them as proudly as any crown during the investiture of her husband as Duke of Suffolk in her right. He had become tender towards her, pleased by the position he had gained through her.

That night they danced before the King and the court as though they were a young married couple. They gambled heavily and drank deeply.

Life was good.

As was expected, the Dukedom came with a price. John Dudley was hungry for his own title and demanded Henry's support. No Englishman had ever held the title of Duke before without royal ties or blood. Now here he was, being named Duke of Northumberland.

He prostrated himself before his King as his titles were read out to him, and he was finally invested with the title.

Frances could practically see his heart leaping to his chest as his Letters Patent were read out. She knew the feeling but felt she had borne it with more grace than he was doing. Of course, she had royal blood in her veins and had expected nothing but greatness her whole life.

That night they feasted again, the swan being prepared especially well.

"You'll turn to fat," Henry teased her, seeing her fill her plate again.

"I will do no such thing." She threw back her head and

laughed. "It wouldn't matter anyways as I can have my coronet adjusted anytime I please."

"That is the sin of gluttony." He tapped her on the nose as though scolding his dog, but his eyes were merry and he kissed her full on the mouth.

"Are you as happy as I am?" she asked him.

"Very much so." He kissed her again and she leaned into his warm embrace, not caring if they could be seen by the court.

～

For all the lands and gifts the King gave away, his treasury was always on the verge of being empty.

Frances decided to quit court and let her husband spend his days in the privy chamber, deciding the fate of the Kingdom. She sought pleasure not work. With her three daughters in tow, she went to stay with Lady Mary at her town home in London.

Despite their religious differences, they remained close friends and Mary loved to spoil her daughters.

"I brought you a gift of pomegranates imported from Spain," Frances said.

"I have gifts for you as well, I hope you shall enjoy your stay here."

Indeed, Mary seemed starved for company. Ever since her brother had forbidden her to have the Mass said in her chapel, she was left very much alone by conservatives wishing to evade notice of John Dudley. Frances looked into Mary's face and was surprised to find a gaunt sickly woman.

Where was the pretty Princess of her youth? The scholar and musician who she had always envied?

"Jane, I shall have you whipped if you send back that dress of gold tissue," Frances hissed at her.

"You cannot prevail upon me. I am not to parade around in finery. It is against the word of God."

Frances raised her hand to her daughter but did not strike.

"You shall do as I say or I shall make sure you are left without tutors or paper and ink. I shall keep you locked in your rooms with nothing to do but contemplate your immortal soul."

Jane looked almost pleased by this prospect but faltered. She could not be without her books.

"Very well, mother. For as the bible—"

"Yes, yes." Frances waved her hands. "I know."

Frustrated as always by her daughter, she went to see if Mary would wish to go riding today or take a barge down the Thames.

CHAPTER EIGHT

1553

"The King looked ill today at dinner," Frances whispered under her breath.

She was in their own bedroom, but still she feared being overheard by some spy.

"He has a cough but the doctors say that the summer weather shall cure him," Henry reassured her.

"My mother was also told the same thing," she reminded him.

"Then we shall hope that God hears the prayers of this county's good Christian people. He has always been a healthy child. He has been still attending council meetings regularly. Smallpox weakened him last summer but he shall rally again."

"And... if he were to... leave this earth?" Frances pressed.

"Lady Mary would inherit."

"Dudley would never allow that to happen and you know it. He fears she would overturn all the religious reforms and return England to Rome."

"There's no use speculating."

Hearing the finality in his voice, Frances dropped the matter. She put on a russet robe and strode out of the room without a glance back.

~

"He's running a fever, pray to God, Frances, that he is spared." Her husband came running into her rooms, pale as a ghost.

"Who? The King?"

"Yes." Henry pulled at his hair. "It is too soon…"

"What?"

"Lady Mary is to come see him, but she does not know. She is not to know of his illness," he changed the subject.

"We would keep this from her?"

"From as many people as we can," he said. "We would not want to cause a panic. Dudley is suggesting we go meet Lady Mary at her home and escort her to Westminster."

"It would be the first time she would be shown this honor. Would it not make her question?"

"You shall be at the head of the ladies."

He seemed to ignore her completely but the thought pleased her.

"We are good friends."

"And that is why she will trust you when you tell her that all is well with the King."

Slowly, she nodded, agreeing to do as he wished, thinking to spare her friend the worry.

As expected, Mary was taken aback by the attention and deference paid to her. She was especially concerned about the kindness shown to her by John Dudley, who had always been an enemy to her. She had thought that the delay of being summoned to see Edward was due to his being angry with her. Frances had to reassure her.

"He has been unwell but nothing to concern yourself over. He asked you to come to his rooms."

"Very well." Mary was as skittish as a cat.

Frances was not with her when she entered the King's rooms, but she heard from the grapevine that they had spent the afternoon talking pleasantly.

~

"Are you once again disobeying me Jane?" Frances slammed her hand on the table between them.

"I shall not marry him."

"You will do what we command," Henry yelled, though this did not seem to scare the young girl one bit. Frances walked around the table to tower over her daughter.

"Before God, I swear—"

Whatever oath she was about to utter was cut short by Frances's slap.

"Be silent or I shall have your tongue cut out of your mouth. I had not realized I had raised such a disobedient child." Frances turned to Henry. "I blame you for this, letting her study all day has given her airs."

"You shall be obedient to us and marry Guildford Dudley."

"No." Her voice was not as sure now.

"Shall we have you beaten until you agree?" Henry was furious his favorite daughter would not bend to his will.

Frances's eyes met Henry's.

"You shall remain locked in your rooms until you come to your senses. Without food or water."

Jane looked aghast but remained resolved to disobey them. Perhaps she thought Frances was bluffing.

Her daughter proved to be made of sterner stuff than her. She endured a day's captivity and her father's temper, which turned violent until Frances prevailed on him to stop. Finally, seeing that they would not relent, she agreed to the betrothal.

Frances was happy plans could go ahead as planned.

The wedding of her eldest daughter would be a triple-wedding, and she would also see her second daughter married to Lord Herbert. The Dudley and the Grey families would be cemented by an alliance, sealed with the inter-marriage of their heirs.

Frances had hoped to have given Jane a better husband than the fourth son of a recently ennobled Duke with no prospects but now she felt Jane deserved even less. She lacked all gratitude for the opportunities her parents had given her.

"Shall King Edward be attending?" Frances thought of the sickly King, pale and withdrawn in his bed.

"No, I don't believe he can, but he has given this union his blessing and is sending jewels and gowns from the royal wardrobe," Henry said.

"He's doing so poorly?"

"I am afraid so."

~

After Easter, the King was still not well and was restricted to his bed. Slowly they moved from Westminster to Greenwich. It was hard for Frances to ignore the rumors.

The citizens of London were not blind to the failing health of the King. Word seemed to spread like wildfire that the King was unwell. Some rumors claimed he had already died and it prompted King Edward to make a public appearance, but his ghostly physic did nothing to silence rumors.

"Jane's marriage cannot be stalled. It must go ahead with all haste," Henry informed her looking up from the letter.

"It is too soon." Frances brushed it aside. Secretly, she was hoping the betrothal would be broken.

"No, Somerset writes to me that preparations shall begin immediately and that she should stay with them at Durham House."

"And you would obey him?" Frances asked, sickened to think her husband was Dudley's lapdog.

"It's for the best. You shall see."

"I wish you would tell me. This wouldn't be the first time you jumped head first into unknown waters."

She could tell he did not appreciate that from the twitch on his forehead, but he said nothing.

~

The ceremonies took place by the end of the month. Frances attributed this to the King's increasing ill health, but it seemed more like a move by Dudley to consolidate power. She almost feared the elderly man. There was an air about him that forced her to look away from him.

She dared not argue with him or show him any disrespect.

When she had heard that Henry had agreed to betroth Jane to Guildford, she had wanted to complain about the insult done to their family. A fourth son in exchange for an heir so close to the throne? But Henry had decided keeping his own council, and there was little she could do without risking Dudley's wrath.

The day of the wedding, the promised clothes arrived at Durham House — the Dudley residence. Frances fingered the precious velvets and tissues. She recognized many as belonging to Anne Seymour, the wife of the fallen Duke.

She chose a silver brocade overcoat to wear. It was embroidered with pearls and tiny white roses. The silver thread danced against the light.

"Jane, you are to wear the purple," she said, spotting her daughter touching a dark black velvet.

"The show of wealth..."

"Jane," Frances said warningly. Her other daughters did not seem to find the wealth displeasing.

Catherine was her prettiest daughter with golden hair and a sweet face. If it wasn't for her tendency to be dower all the time, Jane would be pretty as well. It was her third daughter that she had a hard time seeing.

The girl was an embarrassment to her. They kept saying that she would grow out of her small stature, that she was still just a child, but soon it would be harder to tell this lie. It had been eight years since she had last been with child and she cursed her barrenness. Perhaps it was her punishment for all the pride she had in herself.

Looking away from Mary, she focused on the jewel box, picking a few items out of there before Jane Dudley came to steal the best pieces for herself.

With everyone dressed and ready, they moved to the chapel. Hundreds of people had come to attend these weddings. Everyone had been invited except for the ambassadors and the King's half-sisters. Frances would have liked to see Mary at the wedding, knowing she would have taken joy in seeing these weddings.

The ceremony was simple. There was no muttering in Latin by the priest or any Catholic ceremony. After, the couples were led to the great hall where plate after plate of food was brought out.

Frances watched her children sitting at the table on the dais so everyone could see them. Catherine was blushing and smiling at all the compliments she was receiving, but Jane beside her looked as sour as though she had been fed lemons. Guildford looked less than pleased as well.

Her lips tighten in irritation. Jane should be lucky anyone was taking such an interest in her.

Someone squeezed her hand, and she turned to find Henry had taken his seat beside her.

"Don't worry about her," he said misinterpreting her feelings.

"She will embarrass us if she continues looking as though she was facing her execution."

He laughed and kissed her hand.

"She is young, and she shall learn that God has called her to a great destiny."

Frances thought no more of what he had said as Jane Dudley, parading around with ermine trimming her gown, was approaching.

She had never disliked the woman, but, ever since her husband had taken control of the council, they had fought in a thousand little ways. From who would walk first through the door, to who would draw on the best clothes from the royal wardrobe.

She was no Anne Seymour, but Frances thought she had become just as self-important.

After the wedding night, Jane returned to Suffolk Place with them. It was a small victory for Frances that Jane preferred her company over that of her in-laws. She knew Jane Dudley had pushed for her to remain at Durham House.

Feeling kindly to Jane, she allowed her some freedom and left her to her own devices.

Henry did not seem to care that the couple was ill-suited to one another. He always walked around with a dreamy look on his face. If Frances was any other woman, she would suspect him of being in love.

~

Jane was laughing as she told her what Jane Dudley had told her. Frances was struggling to maintain a calm countenance.

"She said the King has named you his heir?"

Jane nodded. "Can you believe it? She has lost all sense

or is teasing me."

"You should rest, you are looking unwell."

"But shall I have to go to Durham House?"

"Not for now anyways."

Frances was not paying attention to her, she was thinking where Henry could be right now and left her bewildered daughter in her study without a look back.

"Henry!" she called, seeing he was on his horse ready to ride away.

She ran as fast as she could towards him.

"Is something the matter?" He looked past her, worried.

"Jane has told me the most peculiar thing..." She watched his every move like a hawk watching its prey. "Has she been named the King's heir? Is this what the Dudley marriage was all about?"

First, his eyes widened in shock, then his features settled into stony resolution as though he was preparing for a fight. This set her on edge. She grabbed hold of his reins.

"Henry?"

"We cannot talk here." He jumped down from his horse and called over a groom to hold the horse ready for him. "I'll be back shortly."

He pulled Frances along by the arm, but she couldn't be bothered to struggle. With each step, a horrifying thought became more real. Finding a quiet alcove, he stopped and turned to her.

"The King is not expected to last until Christmas. He has altered your uncle's will. He dares not allow Mary to take the throne so he named your male heirs as next in line to inherit the throne."

"But?"

"The matter is complicated." He was trying to brush her away but Frances wasn't having it.

"Tell me now," she commanded in an icy tone she had not used with him since the early days of their marriage.

"The King is concerned and wishes for a male heir to the throne as soon as possible."

"Yes, I am assuming that's why Jane was married so hastily."

"And you know that his health has only declined even more... Jane and her male heirs shall inherit the throne, and if she should die without issue then the throne would go to Catherine."

Frances blinked.

"And me?"

"You shall be the Queen's mother."

"My claim to the throne." She pounded her fists on his chest.

He grabbed them and held her close. "You will renounce it in favor of your daughter. It is the King's wish."

"It is your wish!" she seethed. "Yours and that crook John Dudley."

"Hush, do you want everyone to hear you?"

She took a moment to catch her breath.

"Why would you forsake the throne? I would have had you at my side crowned King," she said, trying her hardest to keep her voice from shaking with emotion.

"Who would support us? We would have too many enemies. The only reason John Dudley is supporting us is to consolidate his power and to see his family married into the royal Tudor line. He will see his son on the throne beside Jane. He would support us for nothing less."

She pulled away from him.

"It is because you are too weak. Even if she is crowned Queen then he will merely hold the reins of power as he did with Edward. He would be in control. Not us."

"It is too late now. I see you aren't seeing sense." He looked away.

But she forced him to look at her.

"Is this what you have been planning all this time? Why wouldn't you have spoken to me sooner?"

"You are my wife. I knew you would be upset and I wanted to spare you. I am your husband and you shall obey me."

"I am not your children to be ordered around. I shall refuse to step aside."

"You cannot. I shall refuse on your behalf if necessary." He was frowning at her as though she was a petulant child he had to discipline. "See sense. We could not have held the throne, but through Jane there is more than just a chance. Dudley holds the council's support. You shall have all the privilege you have always desired."

"But not as Queen."

He nodded. "Not as Queen," he parroted back to her.

He lifted her face towards him; she had not wished him to see the hot angry tears welling up in her eyes.

"My love, you shall see this is all for the best. Tell me I have your support — Jane shall need someone to guide her."

Defeated, she agreed.

Henry bent forward and placed a kiss on her quivering lips. "You see, I have always looked out for what's best for you. I am taking care of this family and ensuring it rises to the greatness it deserves. Now, I must go, Dudley has summoned the Privy Council and Bishops."

She did not even notice him leaving. She supported herself on the stone wall with her right arm to stop from falling to the floor. Once, she had feared being put aside but not like this. Her worst fears had come true, but not perhaps in the way she had imagined.

She suddenly felt robbed.

He had taken her father's title, taken her childhood home and now he had taken her crown too. She had given everything she could to him. He had not risen through his own merit but through hers. Shouldn't she be the one to decide?

Did everyone have such little faith in her that they would prefer her daughter Jane? What had she done to merit such punishment?

Her breath was coming in hard, she knew she mustn't faint. Not here.

Slowly, she made her way to her rooms. Dismissing her ladies and forbidding anyone from disturbing her. She lay on her bed until the late hours of the night.

Her room, illuminated by the light of the moon, casting strange shadows about the room. She thought of her jealousy and hatred of Katherine Willoughby and her sinful happiness at being able to inherit the Dukedom. She touched the mark on her shoulder.

Was some witch's curse flowing through her veins?

Suddenly, she remembered Princess Mary who had always been her friend. Her daughter would be stealing her crown, and she was going to let it happen. Had she ever been truly loyal to her friends? Did she not abandon

Catherine Parr to face the wrath of her uncle alone? Her lists of grievous sins seemed endless. Why should she be surprised that God had decided to punish her in this way? The pain in her head seemed to move to her heart. She felt she was being crushed more and more until she thought she might die on the spot.

She all but crawled to the crucifix hanging on the wall in her bedroom and knelt before it.

"God, forgive me..." she began a lengthy prayer. Her daughter Jane would approve.

When the first signs of light lit her room, she was still on her knees, her voice raspy. She found a dull peace sometime during the long night. The more she prayed, the quieter the voices in her head became. This was all in God's plan. She had no control over any of it. She was but a sinner. The lessons of her childhood repeated themselves over and over again in her head.

In the resulting emptiness of her mind, a thought bloomed.

It was her daughter Jane on the throne, she was standing beside her, looking proud. Jane looked up at her, and, like the benevolent mother she was, she placed a leading hand on her daughter's shoulder. They could find a way to wrestle power away from John Dudley. She could be the guiding influence in her daughter's life.

She thought of her great-grandmother Margaret Beaufort — who signed her name *Margaret Regina*. She had been all but Queen, though she had never worn a crown. Frances could be like her.

By the afternoon, Frances could no longer stand the pain of her parched throat. She rose from the floor and felt reborn. She opened her locked bedroom door to find her ladies waiting outside anxiously.

"G-get me so-me water and food," she ordered.

Once she was better, she would send for Jane. Her daughter would have to go to Durham House.

∾

"She's staying at Chelsea now. Jane Dudley wrote to me and said she was feeling unwell."

Henry sighed. "Well at least she is close at hand. The Privy Council have finally agreed to the King's device for the succession. He is slipping further away from us with each day."

"And the others?"

"They shall fall into line. Dudley has enough money and arms to quell any rebellion."

Frances nodded.

"We have been invited to stay at Syon House in the meantime. I think you and Mary should go. I shall be at court with Dudley."

"Very well," she said, though she thought how horrid it would be to share a roof with Jane Dudley.

When they arrived, Frances found the house quite full of Dudleys and their affinity.

"Welcome, your grace." Jane greeted her.

Both women curtseyed to each other careful not to show more deference to the other.

"I see you have made a merry house here," Frances said, noting the new rich tapestries hanging on the walls, and the fresh rushes.

The household seemed prepared for a celebration rather than one awaiting sad news that must come from court any day now. While the country was anxious over their sickly King, the people in Syon House walked around without a care in the world. Confident of their power and position, no one dared to think of a world where the Dudleys could fall.

Frances thought dryly that they looked like a child itching to receive a gift at any moment. That gift was the Kingdom of England.

She almost felt in the shadows, especially as the Earls of Arundel and Huntingdon arrived, paying every homage to their host.

It was not long before the news that the King had passed made its way around this inner circle of conspirators. Frances watched with hitched breath as more nobles arrived. Finally, her daughter was sent for. Mary Sidney, John Dudley's daughter, was sent to fetch her by barge.

Dressed in a gown of deep red, rings with precious stones on each finger, Frances waited beside her husband at the forefront of the group assembled in the presence hall. Her headdress sparkled with diamonds and rubies, nearly a crown on her head. No one looking at her could see anything but the poise of royalty.

Time seemed to stretch on and she remained frozen in place, her eyes never moving from the door where her daughter would enter from.

Tomorrow she would accompany her daughter to the Tower, carrying her train, and see her crowned in Westminster in only a few days. These thoughts kept her occupied until, finally, Mary Sidney came through the door, Jane following behind her, almost apprehensive.

They greeted her gently, seeing she was already on edge. But the deference shown to her did not put her at ease. Then, almost as if they were one, the congregation knelt.

Jane's protests went unheard as John Dudley, Duke of Northumberland, announced in a loud clear voice that the King had drawn his last breath and named Jane his heir as stated in the King's amendment to his father's will. Jane was Queen.

"God Bless the Queen," the room said as one.

Frances, who had not taken her eyes off her daughter, saw her go white and lose her balance. In an instant, she was at her daughter's side, catching her before she fell to the floor.

"Get a hold of yourself, Jane," she whispered to her.

Jane, still weak and in danger of fainting again, protested loudly that it was her cousin Mary who should inherit. John Dudley protested and reaffirmed that the King had desired her to take the crown. Finally, with some reluctance Jane accepted.

Drinks were passed around and the nobles cheered. Jane was taken out of the room to rally her spirits. She was but a pawn in this game, and her presence was no longer required.

Frances did not sleep that night.

Pride swelled in her chest. She thought of the power she would hold as the Queen's mother. The adoration of the people. She would be influential. The night of penance was forgotten. She would find a way to atone for her sins.

Tomorrow they would process to the Tower and all the world would hear of her triumph.

The next day, she was so elated that she barely heard the flourish of trumpets and the herald's cries.

"Lady Jane Grey is Queen of England."

AFTERWORD

As with all my books, this was a labor of love, written for entertainment.

Frances Grey has been labeled by history as an evil, unfeeling woman.

I wished to explore her character and perhaps shed her in a more positive light.

Please know that while I have done my best to be as accurate as possible, I have embellished facts and created events that likely never happened.

～

Frances Grey would live to see all her hopes and ambitions dashed. John Dudley failed to capture Princess Mary, who had fled to Norfolk and raised an army.

The country, though mostly Protestant by now, felt that it was Princess Mary who was the true heir and rose to support her.

Jane Grey would never leave the Tower and was executed in February of 1554.

She became known to history as the Nine Day Queen and held up as an innocent martyr for the Protestant faith. Frances Grey and her husband became notorious villains in her story. First, by forcing her to wed Guildford Dudley and then by pushing her on the throne.

Instead of speculating on what we can never truly know for certain, I tried to imagine the life of a woman first overshadowed by her mother and then her daughter.

Following her death, Frances's other two daughters met equally tragic ends. One would die in prison following a secret marriage, and the other would die of the plague after a long imprisonment.

Printed in Great Britain
by Amazon